shine on me

shine on me

A NOVEL

A. G. Mojtabai

TriQuarterly Books
Northwestern University Press
Evanston, Illinois

TriQuarterly Books
Northwestern University Press
www.nupress.northwestern.edu

The book's epigraph is from "Israeli Travel: Otherness Is All, Otherness Is Love," in *Open Closed Open: Poems by Yehuda Amichai*, translated from the Hebrew by Chana Bloch and Chana Kronfeld. Copyright ©2000 by Chana Bloch and Chana Kronfeld. Reprinted by permission of Houghton Mifflin Harcourt Publishing Co. All rights reserved.

Printed in the United States of America

10 9 8 7 6 5 4 3 2 1

This is a work of fiction. Characters, places, and events are the product of the author's imagination or are used fictitiously and do not represent actual people, places, or events.

Library of Congress Cataloging-in-Publication Data
Names: Mojtabai, A. G., 1937– author.
Title: Shine on me : a novel / A. G. Mojtabai.
Description: Evanston, Illinois : TriQuarterly Books / Northwestern University Press, 2016.
Identifiers: LCCN 2016032145 | ISBN 9780810134171 (pbk. : alk. paper) | ISBN 9780810134188 (e-book)
Classification: LCC PS3563.O374 S54 2016 | DDC 813.54—dc23
LC record available at https://lccn.loc.gov/2016032145

For Chitra and Ramin, Joaquin, Shahrzad, and Cyrus, again and always

Have you only a single blessing, father?
Bless me, me also, father!

—Gen. 27:38

And I said to myself: Everyone is attached to his own lament
as to a parachute. Slowly he descends and slowly hovers
till he touches the hard place.

—Yehuda Amichai, *Open Closed Open*
(translated from the Hebrew by Chana Bloch and Chana Kronfeld)

Contents

A Note to the Reader

Here's the deal: whoever keeps his hands longest on one of the dealer's brand new pickup trucks owns it and gets to drive it away . . .

This book is focused on a contest sponsored for several years by an auto dealership in Longview, Texas. I learned of it through S. R. Bindler's 1998 documentary *Hands on a Hard Body*. The film has had quite an afterlife, serving also as the source of a musical theater production with the same title. I caught up with its New York theater production in April of 2013, long after my own manuscript was set. There was, as expected, some inevitable overlap due to our shared factual base, but the contest which generated all three versions (documentary, musical theater, and novel) emerges with stark differences in mood and meaning in each case. I think there is interest in this very triplication. Clearly, the original contest, although intended perhaps as nothing more than an advertising gimmick for the dealership, is fertile ground for many reflections.

My version is considerably darker than that of the film or the (resolutely upbeat) musical. However, as proven by later events and the dealer's decision to terminate the contest, my more somber version of character and event is not an altogether fanciful or arbitrary one.

Among the real-life components of my account are some of the gestures from the actual contestants. I have quoted the final comment of the winner and (with minor adjustments) built on the basic setup of the contest as devised by the sponsoring auto dealership.

But, again let me remind the reader: my tale is fiction. The way of fiction, with its privileged access to inner lives normally kept hidden, struck me as well fitted to a contest of standing and waiting in which, for long stretches of time, it seems as if "nothing is happening."

Writing this as fiction, I have felt free to take liberties with chronology and factual detail in the source event. There are many instances. To name but a few: I have shifted the venue from East to West Texas, upgraded the pickup to a double cab version and, although the contest was terminated in 2005, included references to the first *Happy Feet* film released in 2006. Electronic devices mentioned belong to the '90s, the early years of the contest, to a time and place in which cell phones were few and far between and MP3s and smart phones yet to become ubiquitous. In any case, the kind of realism I strive for is not literalism. Finally: It must be understood in reading any fiction, even one based on a real event, that the characters are mosaics of traits and gestures observed in real life from many disparate sources, then dreamed-over, and *into,* by the author, drawing from imagination and self-interrogation. The author alone is to blame for what comes of this mixing.

shine on me

1

Clare: From the Sidelines

When the ground under her feet surged and fell away Clare knew she wasn't going to last. Then dizziness took over, and a raging thirst, then her left hand started to twitch, a separate creature with a mind of its own. What's worse, she caught herself calling the hand "Selma" after a cousin she'd never liked, her irritation rising to such a pitch that she burst out with "Quit that!" (speaking to her hand), causing the gal standing on her left, who'd done nothing to deserve it, to flinch. Her tag read *Sheree*, that's how she spelled it, though with Clare so whipped and bleary-eyed, the name could easily be mistaken for Selma—it could be explained.

But this was the final straw. Clare decided it was time to take Selma out of the game and deliberately lifted one hand, then the other, freeing both hands to be able to peel off the gloves.

Quitting, as it turned out—loosening her hands from the gleaming metal of the hood—was easier than she ever imagined. All but blinded by its luster to start, she was no longer dazzled. And she'd shuffled back to her chair, flumping herself down with relief.

There are unsold cars everywhere Clare looks. There's a girl, a shadow amid shadows, weaving between the rows, the lumps of darkness and scattered gleams. Clare has to strain to keep her in focus.

Clare's pretty sure she recognizes her as a player, one of the former players.

Looks lost . . .

But—so?

So? What am I supposed to do about it?

Clare leans back, stretches . . . *Allow yourself. It's vacation time. Remember to savor it.* She's earned her rest. The girl is no part of her responsibility.

The girl must be quitting for good now, looking for the way out. Yet she'd seemed primed to beat most of the competition through the early rounds. Stroking on lipstick and eyeliner with one hand while guiding herself by her reflection in the hood, she'd seemed cool as a cucumber to start. Seemed like someone who could cut, shuffle, and deal one-handed, no problem. What happened?

It must have slipped her mind where she was. Three others had quit one after the other, opening up a little more space to move and she'd claimed it, sliding restlessly back and forth, massaging the metal with two hands, both hands joined to the truck.

That went on for a while.

Until she lost it. Started housekeeping, dusting and polishing that gleaming, immaculate hood, as she lifted one hand, replaced it, then lifted the other, and then—an instant is all it took—let go of both. Poor thing: in the end she simply forgot what this was all about.

. . . *Still at it*—the girl's stalling and doubling back on herself. Getting nowhere. *Dazed apparently . . .* Clare puts it to herself: *How can you just sit here and watch?*

And at last, because no one else is stirring, Clare picks herself up, doing her best to balance evenly on both feet, taking a couple of deep breaths first—*to stabilize*—before starting to go after the girl. The ground is still rocking a bit, although steadier than before.

Testing . . . Clare places her feet with extreme care.

The heat clings, even now.

No question, the girl is lost. She's still backing and forthing through the rows of display cars, pacing like a creature caged, unable to believe in her release. Clare doesn't think she's bent on damage, though—too light-headed probably for anything like that.

Clare would have called to her by name had the girl not torn off her nametag right after throwing down her gloves. So all Clare can do is holler: "Hey! You, there! Number 7—you all right?" Feels like there's sand in her throat when she tries to shout.

The reply, if there is one, is too faint to catch.

"Where you heading?" Clare asks.

"Home," the girl says.

"Where's that?" Clare is closing the distance now.

"Don't know," she answers, her voice wobbling.

They stand, paused for the instant, flanking opposite fenders of the same hatchback.

"Maybe if you go through your pockets." She's wearing cargo pants, pockets up and down. "Bet there's something to remind you in one of them. Keys, shopping list, something. Bound to be."

She pats a couple of the high pockets, comes up with a broken comb and lipstick. Anyone can tell she isn't making a serious effort.

"Nope. Not even a button," she says.

"Maybe you left the keys in. Where's your car?" Clare persists. "What kind of car?"

"Old."

"Oldsmobile?"

"No, no, just old!"

"You remember your name, at least?"

"Glad . . . I think . . ."

"Is that Gladys?"

With her lips moving silently, she seems to be trapped in some sort of dream, not fully asleep but not truly awake.

"Well, let's get you back to where someone *does* remember," Clare suggests, making the mistake of stretching her hand across—

"Hey!"

When the girl bolts—makes a dash for open space—she's too fast to follow. And it's happened again: Clare can no longer trust her feet. Just no feeling at all. She has to let her go.

All she can do is stand and look on as the girl toils up the feeder road bordering the car lot, heading for the main highway. An empty flatbed hauler rumbles past, then a cattle truck passes, a lone bleating cry trailing like a long banner after it. Then . . . nothing. Clare notices a man in uniform mounting a motorbike to take up the chase.

And now, thank goodness, he's gaining on her. *Got her!* Clare is free to limp back to her chair and treat herself to that promised recovery time. She knows she hasn't handled this incident well, but she shouldn't have tried to handle it at all. Anyhow, from here on out, the girl is somebody else's problem. She's no part of Clare's business, never was.

There's the buzzy sound of the P.A. system warming up, then three blasts of a whistle and the amplified voice of the dealer: "Return to your positions, please. If you want to be counted." Clare can no longer be counted; she has no intention of sticking around that much longer. She keeps telling herself: *That truck—the so-called hard body—was never hard, never solid, never really real,* yet she follows the dealer's voice, tugged along, as though leashed to it.

It was never a matter of life or death for Clare. *Would have been nice, of course . . .* She'd have traded it in for a bundle. *Sure could've used the money . . .*

She's still curious to learn how things might turn out, though not prepared to camp out here for the days and nights and hours it might require. *One more round; two at most . . .* She'll rest while she watches. She needs to rest. Then, no matter what happens, she's on her way. She's free to go any time, nobody to say good-bye to, nobody likely even to notice. Whenever she's ready, she'll gather up her things and vanish like all the others who've quit or been disqualified have done. *It's the strangest thing—the way players disappear, melt away, simply evaporate.* Excepting Clare herself, of course, and the girl she'd been trying to rescue. *She seemed so lost* . . . Clare can't remember her name, but the girl, herself, sounded none too sure of it.

2

Trew: What He's Noticed So Far

A toddler, pointing to the rising sun, cries out "Moon! Moon!" No one bothers to correct her.

Another morning—can it be?

Trew Reade flips through his notes from the start of the contest. He uses a pocket recorder for live interviews but habits die slowly and most of the time he finds it easier jotting things down in a notebook, the old way.

He underlines:

> *Each plans to win*
> *All but one will lose*

He has noted the handing out of T-shirts with the player's number in front, dealer's logo on back, and the thickwhite cotton gloves they must wear to preserve the shine of the metal. Each player had to fill out a nametag, a stick-on label, but, what with everybody sweating so, the names have not been sticking for long.

He's made note of the curious entrance theme:

> *gathering music—*
> *tapping at gallop tempo*
> *hop-shuffle-chop to whistle and snare drum*

Where had he heard this music before? Movie? Probably. Must've been with one of the grandkids . . . *Happy Feet*, was it?

Strange sense of humor, whoever picked it out—nothing around here suggests penguins frolicking on ice. Aside from the fact that it's hot as Hades, even the happiest feet will not be happy as the hours wear on.

they circle round the pickup
like musical chairs

Wherever the music stopped there they remained for the entire first round. But after that there's been no music—only whistle blasts.

Scrambling for position at the start, most aimed for the hood even though this meant standing shoulder to shoulder. A few angled in sideways. It couldn't have been pleasant (the jostle of elbows and shoulders, the body heat) for people unused to the press of crowds. But now, as the competition thins out, the realization seems to be spreading that the best spots are not in the front but in the back, around the bed. The bed is covered, flat as a tabletop, holding securely whatever they might bring along—listening devices, magazines, and such—to help pass the time. The hood's more photogenic, but too smooth and sloping; hands, even gloved hands, are liable to slide there. No one who has a choice in the matter opts for the door panels—the wrist must be bent at an unnatural angle to insure contact. And, anyway, as more players leave there's no need for anyone to stand there.

The truck is the still point, the axis around which the players turn, loopier and loopier as they go, round after round.

Layout—

two lots & a covered showroom
contest held in partially cleared lot
canopy over players by day folded up by night
to catch whatever breeze

Daytime, there's usually more audience than available cover, so most of those left out in the open bring beach umbrellas.

By chance?—

player selection: Lots drawn for 25—22 showed up
from pool of how many? Must CHECK
first round placement pure chance (see notes)

First to quit—

starting out, they admit to being spooked
by same question—will it be me?

it's Ted Sims @ 31st hr
laughing to the end
talking up "silly powder" and "wacky tobacky"
acting like he's on something but they
checked for that

threw down gloves kicked the wheel
hurried away—"Can't take no more!"
wdn't say another word

After him, it must've seemed easier to quit. Four followed in the
next round.

Need?

forklift operator, ranch-hand, grocery checkout clerk,
janitor, manicurist,
feedlot attendant, receptionist, cement finisher
2 "looking for work"
they talk about needing a pickup
for "hauling things" & how car won't hack it

"Gotta have that truck!"—all say same thing.

One of the players admits to being in it for the fame.
"Fame?" Trew knows he shouldn't, but can't let that pass without comment: "What—*here?*"

Misc—

the truck is dark red stage roped-off
red white & blue chalk mark borders of staging area

free drinks from dealer

Cans of a drink called "Buster's," a name he never heard of, are ready to hand. One of those new high energy varieties. It's a promo, free of charge. So: they'll be "riding for the brand"—for Buster's and, of course, for the dealership.

"Ordeal" was the word his wife used during their last phone conversation. Trew wasn't—still isn't—ready to call it that, although it *is* wearing.

He had to admit that he had no idea how long it would take: last year, he's been told, it came to well over ninety hours. One of the players—announced at the start that he was going to stand there till he dropped dead, so everyone else might as well quit right then and go home and be comfortable. That just fired up everyone else and they stuck all the harder. But he did win.

"But, hon, if it's going to go on for that long, why not call for backup? Nobody expects—"

"If I have to, but I can catnap, I can pick the times. It's interesting."

"You call that interesting—people standing around *doing nothing*? Staring at a dumb pickup truck?"

"It isn't the truck." He's still trying to explain it to himself. It's the intensity of the *wanting* that surrounds it that's got him hooked.

What Trew remembers best from the contest so far is this image: a trickle of wetness down the inside of a man's bare leg. The damp spot under him he tried to cover with his shoe. It happened only minutes before a break was called, but apparently the man couldn't wait.

He'd been holding on, unnaturally rigid. The other players, focused on hands, not feet, seemed not to notice. By the next round, the man was gone, disappeared. No one asked after him.

Trew hasn't bothered to follow up, or to record the incident— he knows it would never be printed. He's a pragmatist, a professional, has been a reporter for decades.

"You're not getting overinvolved, are you?" Heather kept at it.

"Not a chance! I'm only a spectator here, after all."

"You were only a spectator before."

"A different situation, totally different. This is harmless."

"You sure? Honey? Remember what the doctor said about your blood pressure. What you promised. It's only a story—'tomorrow's fish wrapper' you use to say. Is it worth your health? You won't last to retirement going on like you did before."

She reminded him of what she'd packed for him in the way of spare clothes, toothbrush, electric shaver—

"How about floss?" he teased. "You forget floss?"

"That, too," she said, dead sober, and warned him to avoid fast food (uselessly—there's no other kind to be had nearby). He promised to "eat healthy" once he got back, to lose twenty pounds in the next three months while he's at it. And he promised to call as soon as he started heading back if the hour was at all decent.

Oh, and another thing: she wanted him to pick up two big sacks of mulch at Walmart on his way back. Could he remember that?

He promised to remember.

3

Sheree: Headache

It's the sixty-fifth hour with fewer than half of them still standing. Already it's been, like, forever. She's got a honey of a headache.

Things rocking a little.

Starting to float . . .

Keep your hand on it—all that's required. Just the one hand, how hard can that be?

It's the sixty-sixth hour. More standing room each time: they slide along the metal, stretching out. Sheree's feeling filthy with tiredness. She's not dreaming (she *knows* she's not) but everything's gone queer on her. Like the sound of a door singing somewhere as it swings, or the lamps, tasseled, trailing threads of light. She can make the lights swirl by moving her free hand.

She blinks hard to make sure she's seeing what she thinks she's seeing: a young mother in the audience holding her baby's fist to her mouth, nibbling the tiny nails, trimming them while the baby sleeps.

Bev, the gal standing on her right, the one who's so super-sure she's going to win, because God sees her need and hears the prayer chain that's cheering and pulling for her, is busy kissing her guardian angel. Too much kissing, looks like the gold paint's starting to flake off. She's got quite a spread—with prayer cards, one of those clunky old-fashioned tape recorders, and a stack of tapes she's been mouthing the words to, sometimes just lip-synching in silence, or sometimes (obnoxiously on purpose?) out loud. She won't be able to turn the page in the Bible she's got open in front of her, not with gloves on, the pages are too thin.

As for Sheree—all she's got is the Lord's Prayer on a stretched penny and her lucky rabbit's foot on a keychain. Simply hedging her bets, she doesn't rely on charms and trinkets. She'll come through—because she's *got* to—standing on her own two feet, not leaning on anybody else, be it guardian angel, or only human. Just how she's always been.

Now Bev's mouthing something churchy, not too loud, but feeling it so hard that her eyes are squinched shut. It's risky closing your eyes here for *any* reason. Somebody ought to clue her in. But, of course, it's to everybody's advantage that no one does.

4

Gib: Planning Ahead

If he'd gone in for any military outfit it would be the Marines. He's got the goods, he *knows* he has, he's got the *cojones—and the discipline*—even though they turned him down for one or two "smart-ass answers."

In the Marines it's boots over everything. Here, it's mind over matter. *Same principle, though.* He has the desire and the power. He claims the prize already by the law of attraction. As if magnetized, as if fastened by strong cords, his hands are pulled down, drawn to the hood.

Perfect the power—ignore the pain. Filter everything else out. Never mind how many fallen away by now.

Three things matter: snacks, shoes, attitude. They're all paying off. Starving the old bod helps. When it's over there'll be ample time to enjoy Big Mac with all the trimmings—fries, slaw, jumbo shake—but for now it's protein bars, tasting every bit like dog kibble. Coffee and coke must be sugarless. Last thing he needs would be a sugar rush, one of those quick fixes that fizzle out in a flash. He's sampled the high energy Buster's beverage they're handing out for free here, doesn't trust it a bit. It's full of caffeine and sugar and damn knows what else. He'll stick with what he knows.

Food is important but attitude is key. What with parole fees, court costs, child support, he *must* win, no ifs, buts, or maybes. So it's settled: he's gonna win. *Gotta—gonna.* Already Gib sees himself snapping the ignition, the motor springing to life; his imagined hands move caressingly, tracing the arc of the steering wheel as his actual hands trace a matching arc over the surface of the hood. *Better quit that now.* He knows there's serious competition standing right alongside of him. *Not Ken—Bev.* The gal that keeps on singing and praying, annoying the hell out of him. And taking up all that space with her doodsies, way too much space. With each break she keeps adding on: a woodcarving of praying hands, a cross of horseshoe nails welded together. It's not as if the lady's simply staking out territory, her portion of the hood that should be no more than two foot square, it's more like she's establishing a kingdom, or queendom: *here be castles, here be gardens . . .*

So . . . Where was he?

First off: attitude. He's got it. He's not one to tiptoe through life. *Second: snacks*: fasting or stinting the old bod helps to focus. No meat (at all!) and as little water as tolerable—no need to be pissing or swelling up with it before breaks.

Shoes: sneakers (unlaced), sweat socks. *Oh-so important.* Should be old sneakers, tried, tested, true, sagged with use. And to think that two of the other players started out in fancy cowboy boots with stacked heels and pointy toes! They're both long gone, of course.

About Bev. . . *Let her waste her energy. Simply tune her out.* He can do it.

His focus is steady: looking ahead. He's a planner. He's come for the truck, and he won't be leaving without it.

5

Manuel: Pair of Old Shoes

Big-mouths, that's all they are. Manuel knows how to outlast them. *Just ignore them.* He's tough, like his *padres*. His *abuelo* was a *Penitente*. Not many people know what that means anymore. Few knew even back then. *Los Hermanos De Penitentes.* It was *muy secreto*. Holy week, the old man would leave the family to join them.

The *Penitentes* had a meeting house, a *morada*. Like a big cube, with only a smoke hole, no windows, and a door always kept locked. From the time he was a child, Manuel wondered what went on there; he knew it was a very big deal, but when he asked no one would tell him.

Once, he'd seen men bowing, bowing and walking backwards out the door, a few scraping the ground on their knees all the way, that's how Manuel knew there was the Blessed Sacrament inside.

Easter, they'd have a procession and whup themselves bad. One got to carry the cross and be tied to the cross. Tied and lifted up. It was a great honor. And if one of them died on the cross the honor was most great.

That's what happened to his *abuelo*. He died and was buried and the family didn't know till after it was over. Only his shoes were left to tell what they could. Somebody must of come while the family was sleeping and left them on the doorstep.

Pair of old shoes, all that was left of him. . . . .

Manuel would never stop seeing those black shoes with their slanting heels and battered soles. Their mouths were open wide, yet their secrets remained hidden, shut inside. Or maybe not, not completely shut, for they'd been carefully placed at a certain angle, with their backs to the door. They were pointing outwards, and wasn't pointing a way of telling—*por allá, over there, that way, out in the desert*—telling in their own way, as much as they could?

"*Mi abuelo* was one tough one . . . He was a *Penitente*." Manuel is embarrassed—shocked, really—to catch himself saying the words aloud. He needn't worry, though. No one notices; no one is listening.

And, anyway, none of these *babosos* standing around the truck would have the least idea what he's talking about.

6

Vince: Lens

Rise straight up: over the heads of the seven still standing.

Centering, slow on: the moon.

Full moon.

Down-shot: slow take. Eye level of parked cars and pickups, family clusters. Long shot: new cars row on row, the dealer's sign. Pause. Hold three beats on billboard, frame:

KEEP YOUR HAND ON IT!
HARDBODY GIVEAWAY CONTEST

Formal shot: players still in the running. Moving clockwise: #8 (Bev), #11 (Gib), #9 (Sheree), #17 (Dan), #20 (Josh), #21 (Ken), #12 (Manuel). The seven stand apart, equidistant, rayed out like the spokes of a wheel.

Reverse spin, go with the wheel: #12 . . . 21 . . . 20 . . . 17 . . . 9 . . . 11 . . . 8 . . .

Down-shot: hands on truck. Panning.

Continuing down-shot. In detail: weight shifting from foot to foot. Frame: castoff shoe, mateless. (Point this a little.) Yes!

Full in on dropped glove. Tighten.

Pull out, away into crowd. Wide shot: lawn chairs, strollers, watchers, sleepers. Panning, then in and out. Breeze blowing up, loose things drifting—

Back: the laughing begins . . .

7

Sheree: Sticking with It

What's so funny?

Bev takes a long look round at the rest of them, then tosses back her head and yelps "woo, wooo—whoo" and starts barking like a pup; and Sheree—she's rocking and heaving with trying to hold in.

Sheree has no idea what started them laughing but it seems to be spreading now, one to the next, coming in leaps and jags. She tries faking a cough so as not to join them.

She's afraid of how catching it is. If one of them yawns, she'll start too, simply by power of suggestion. That would be the last thing she needs. She's been fading in and out. Breechey thoughts, like "breechey cattle" poking their heads through a drift fence, loosening the wires. Loosening everything.

When she tried the Buster's beverage they'd been handing out for free, it was even worse, all she got from it was a jolt of energy that fizzed out fast and a bad case of heartburn that lingered on. She never passes up free anything—seems like she never learns.

She keeps drifting . . .

Asleep while standing? Yes, it can be done—she's been doing it, though brokenly, in snatches. Earlier, she'd spotted a man in the audience sleeping with lids wide apart, head pitched sideways, his mouth like an open drain. Was he dreaming? Could you dream without first closing your eyes, giving some sort of permission?

When Sheree shuts her eyes for even a fraction of a second, she sees something—not a full dream, no story to it, just an eyeful of—whatever. What she saw and heard last (laughter in the background?) was a man with a leaf-blower, chasing a leaf, a single solitary leaf. She knew full well, even while watching the leaf skipping down the street, that it wasn't something actually happening in the waking world.

She's got to stay focused. *Got to.* She *needs* this truck—not the pickup itself but what it will fetch. It's what the truck *means—not*: *maybe* I'll graduate, *but*: *for sure.* Twenty-six now, she knows time is running out. She needs the truck to be able to go to school full time, hassle-free; that "bright future" she's been promised (and not yet caught a glimmer of) hangs on a college degree.

Got rocks in her socks, feels like. *Ignore it—*

She would, if only Number 8—Bev—would quit driving her nuts! The animal sounds she's making remind Sheree how much she misses the sweet soft hum of her little tiger cat. And maybe that's the hum coming from what she thought was a leaf blower in the dream just before.

Her name is Baby Cat ("B. C." for short), and it fits the creature like a glove. She spends most of her time either hanging out in the broom closet or clinging to the bedclothes.

Roommate's looking after her so that shouldn't be a worry.

Bev's still at it—venting, ventilating. Must ease her someway.

Will this night ever pass?

8

Trew: A Reporter's Story

His name's always been a joke.

"Great name for the business," the managing editor said right off the bat. "Direct from Central Casting. Born to report." It only took the one interview: Trew was hired on the spot. And he was given a byline right away.

What Trew remembers best from that first meeting was the editor's desk ornament—a clear Lucite replica of an open book with its title turned to the viewer:

MY LIFE STORY
By Bob Baxter,
Managing Editor

The open pages were blank. What were you expected to make of it? Surely he didn't mean to suggest a life empty of event? More likely, it was Baxter's way of saying that his life was perfectly transparent, an open book—

—which proved to be far from the truth. Two years ago, Baxter became a guest of the government. He's in the pen at present. ("Eating our tax dollars, sucking on the Federal tit," in newsroom parlance.) Seems Baxter had been busy on the side, up to his neck in some sort of Ponzi scheme. All those reporters around him itching for a story, and not one of them had an inkling!

That Lucite book of Baxter's *should* have been fair warning. Surface and substance were rarely the same; transparency could be the most cunning of masks. Yet, as Trew was to learn from practical experience, however doggedly he worked to ferret out the facts, the momentum of breaking news (always something new), deadlines, and cutoffs for reasons of space, routinely got in the way and dictated the shape of the story. And there were other pressures. Sometimes he felt that he was not so much writing a story as negotiating it, haggling for every inch of print and even for content. What's worse—even more compromising—he wonders how often he's come to simply avoid the hassle by making the anticipated adjustments on his own before ever submitting the story. But, then again—*isn't this part of learning to be a professional?* That's how he squares it with himself at least. *You can't fight everything.*

Being assigned the city beat meant covering crime scenes, commissioners' meetings, school boards, and local elections, as well as courthouse proceedings, trials and appeals. When he shifted to the police beat, part of his assignment took him to the death house in Huntsville to witness the send-offs. Texas kept him busy and, after he was asked to become a stringer for the Associated Press, his reputation spread beyond the state. He had to admit that he liked his smattering of fame; it gave him an opportunity to be heard—plus, a little extra on the monetary side never hurt—although it wasn't long before he realized that no recognition or payment could compensate for the toll he paid in sleepless nights or the tremor that gradually overtook his writing hand. His motives weren't pure (*were motives ever?*) yet they weren't entirely, or even largely, self-serving. He could have refused the executions, but reasoned: *If this is what we do, someone has to record it. To let it be known.*

When exactly was it that his role as witness began to feel like that of an accomplice? *A feeling, not a fact—not rational,* as Trew repeatedly reminded himself.

So he'd stayed with it as long as he could stand it, reporting from the death house, bearing his crumb of witness for the human ant-heap. It was too much—it was not enough.

Strange to say, it was not a flawed "procedure" that brought him to finally quit, but one that was technically perfect, without a glitch. Not a heave, not a cough, not a sputter. The prisoner had declined to make a final statement. His crime was vicious, his guilt never in question. The execution process was as smooth and effi-cient as putting a pet to sleep.

It was time: he'd stayed on the assignment for more years than any other reporter, bar none. The only surprise was his transfer to Features, well away from the blare of big ink news, at his own re-quest. If anyone was disappointed at the abrupt close to his prom-ising career, it remained unvoiced. It was only Trew himself, and only at moments, when his withdrawal struck him as a failure of nerve.

In any case, Trew is out to pasture now. He'd thought of this as recovery time at first—not a permanent retreat. It's grown on him, though. And he still has hopes of writing something of note, someway, on his own, sometime.

His writing hand has been steadier since the transfer. The trem-or (for which his doctor never found an organic cause) is no longer a quaking; it's still there, but muted now, hardly noticeable to any-one who hasn't been alerted to it beforehand. But Trew, himself, is never allowed to forget. He frequently drops things, his grasp no longer firm and decisive. And, known only to himself, there's some residual numbness in the heel of his palm and fingertips. He's defi-nitely lost feeling in that hand. Fortunately, it's just the one hand affected, although it happens to be the one he writes with.

Be that as it may . . . He covers the counties these days, lo-cal events like this one. Seems sometimes like he's moved from Death-the-Real-Thing to Life-the-Game, from hard focus to soft. It's a trade-off. He puts in more miles but the stress is way less, no question. He doesn't get bogged down in endless retrospection, taking himself to task, as he used to, about a question he forgot to ask or an extra witness unvisited. The story doesn't repay that kind of attention. And it turns out he actually prefers hanging around in the boonies to being out and about in the city. "Getting to know every dog and cat on a first name basis," as he likes to say. Away from the punishing pace, all those egos colliding and crashing, a safe distance from the City Desk and Aiden's hammering away at every least thing.

Last week he'd covered a grocery sacking tournament in a town outside Lubbock. When he first heard of the contest, he'd been tempted to laugh it off, but, after interviewing the champion sacker (best on "structure," though not the fastest) he'd learned a few things and passed them on to his readers. Like making a "wall of protection" with the canned goods at the bottom of the sack and placing the lighter soft stuff inside that wall, or insulating the ice cream and frozen food by surrounding them with napkins and toilet paper. *Who knew?*

Has he ever made that atom's worth of difference he once thought—hoped—he might? The question haunts him. True— he'd started the ball rolling on the story of Lee Somers, an innocent man put to death by the state; but innocent people were still being put to death. In what he calls his "personal life," Trew knows he's never lived, or loved, at full stretch. He doesn't spend all that much time regretting the fact, yet imagines that he might someday. Come a day when he'd want to have wanted more. Something more . . . What that "something more" would be, whether it even exists, he's not sure.

Right now, even now, he can't forget the death house, there's still this humungous weight he needs to get off his chest . . .

Painting and repainting the walls of the execution chamber (on the advice of a psychologist) to a "soothing" green did little to alter things. Nor did it ease matters much that the drug dispensing apparatus and operator remained hidden behind a one-way mirror so that all you could see was an IV tube trailing from a small square opening lower down in the wall. It did help—a bit—that the curtain was only opened after the IV needle was successfully inserted (after antiseptic was carefully applied to the injection site); if there was a struggle to find a vein, that was something he did not have to witness.

Most of the condemned men were black men or brown, had little schooling, came from broken families, the wrong side of town. Innocent, or guilty, or swept along—who could say with the necessary certainty? Unable to afford their own lawyers, they'd relied on court-appointed public defenders who were overburdened and cash-strapped, uncaring or careless. Trew studied the numbers but, after presenting them to the editorial staff, was greeted with: "We *know* this. Is life unfair? You bet. Tell us something new." All he could do was to keep on witnessing for as long as he could bear it, writing up the executions one by one, keeping a blank numerical tally, a sum total of completions, relying on the condemned man's last words to do the rest.

That was standard operating procedure, the "execution protocol," providing a pause for a final statement before the drugs begin to flow or the switch was thrown. Although some prisoners opted for silence, there was always the opportunity to have a say—to be listened to for once. Some professed innocence with their last breaths. Others begged forgiveness. Again and again you'd hear: "I'm not the same man anymore." Many were eager to end the years of waiting and appeal, wanting simply to get it over with, release from prison on any terms; this had become the only way out. Some claimed to be homesick for heaven and thanked the members of the tie-down team, the men who had so swiftly and efficiently strapped them in. Some thanked the warden, though often bitingly.

As for the official reports, there was a little of what the transcriber called "Allah mumbling" which remained untranslated. In English, the four-letter words would not be written into the record and, anyway, could not be printed in a family newspaper. These curses were to be expected—but there were, in far greater measure, blessings—words of hope to those prisoners still waiting on the row and reminders to their families to hug the little ones at home, words of farewell: "Keep strong. Hold your heads high . . . Be seeing you. I'll be waiting on the other side." Then the warden would tip his glasses—that was the signal.

Sometimes the prisoner tried to communicate what he was experiencing to the last threshold of awareness. "It's coming" . . . "It's overwhelming." Some said they could "taste it"—

"This is for real," one spoke in an amplified whisper. His head turned, and he stared right at Trew, as if speaking his last words in confidence only to him: "I feel my heart going . . ." Their eyes locked. Trew had to cough and face away, feeling his own heart stutter between beats.

Some deaths were easier than others. The serial killer in for a string of gruesome murders showed not a shred of remorse.

A white man, pale and narrow-shouldered, with wire rim specs, he seemed well suited to his job as an accountant, but a highly implausible murderer. "Nobody's bulletproof," he explained. "Might *think* they are. I taught them different." Then he smiled beatifically as he urged the warden to "pull the trigger" and wished "peace, true peace" to everyone invited to this occasion.

One prisoner, who suffered from a lisp and facial tic, sent out a written statement beforehand, to make sure that each word counted. "I'm innocent," he began. He'd been waiting for eleven years for this moment. Trew missed some of the words as they were being spoken, but he had the man's speech in hand: "My truth will last out your truth. I have no kin, no friend. No fear. Go ahead, Warden, give them what they want. You don't want me here and I don't want to be here. Take me away from this place. Go ahead. Finish it off. I'm ready."

A few chose to sing their last words—unmelodious scraps of country-westerns or hymns. One man sang something in Latin, letting everyone know that once upon a time he'd been an altar boy. All Trew can remember are the rhymes: *hominum, terminum, dominum* . . .

And yet, despite all his death penalty misgivings, Trew persists in thinking it a privilege to have your last words listened to and recorded. He actually envies it in a way. He wanted, *needed—still needs*—words carefully considered, words passed on as an inheritance to those left behind. Something more than the usual silence and the tacitly understood "It was fun while it lasted."

He had only to recall his dad's last words . . .

"That nurse has the cleanest nostrils I've ever seen," he'd said— and spoke no more.

It would not do!

Of course, no one in the family had ever dreamed this would be his dad's final say. He'd gone into the hospital for minor surgery. The nurse in question had just stepped out of the room.

Two orderlies entered then, loaded his dad onto a gurney and taken off on a fast glide. It was all over before they knew it.

That was the last Trew saw of his dad alive. His family had always been "non-affiliated" and at the scattering of the ashes, friends and family did their best to avoid any trappings of a traditional graveside ceremony, each of them straining to say something original, something amusing to remember, but Trew felt certain that "dust unto dust" was on everyone's mind.

At the prison death house, people wept and prayed. The family members of the victims spoke of "closure." Once in a while—but not as often as people might suppose—one of the watchers would faint. He'd seen people on the victims' side clap or give one another high-fives when it was over. That didn't happen often, but it did happen. As for Trew, he'd be ready to split as soon as the snoring (in the new improved way) or the thrashing (in the old days) ended. His deadline gave him a perfect excuse to scram . . .

It's close to two A.M. now. Hours and hours yet to get through . . . His watch is slow, must be the battery running down. He carries a spare: he'll change it. The metal expansion band is nipping his wrist—normally, Trew takes it off when he goes to bed. There's really no need for a watch here, what with the hours, minutes, seconds, fractions of seconds continually flashing on the big screen. He'd be lost without a wristwatch, though. It's another one of those habits.

Right now he's struggling to get back on assignment, wondering: *What have I missed? How many down?*

When he asks the cameraman for the local television affiliate (name's Vince, if memory serves) what's new, he's equally blank, as if he might've been napping. His camera's aimed and ready, though, perched on its tripod. "Just waiting for something to happen," he explains.

But, no sooner done explaining, he's on his feet, fiddling with the focus on his lens. And now he's shooting. When he's done Trew reminds him that he'd just said nothing was happening.

"What roused you?"

"Background . . . interesting . . . Have a look."

He lets Trew peek through his viewfinder. Caught in its frame: a boy, holding what looks like a cicada by one wing, using the insect as a fan, the other wing beating frantically against the boy's cheek.

"Trying to stir up a breeze with a tiny little thing like that— imagine!" Trew exclaims. He feels compelled to say something to keep the words moving and mime interest—anything to keep himself awake.

T WO A.M.: This is one of those times when if you stare at a blank wall it stares back at you. Because nothing is happening. *Really, nothing.* Only a cleaning woman, a Latina with a long braid down her back, rattling her buckets, brooms, and mops, moving through the crowd of sleepers and watchers, stooping to gather loose trash on her way to the washroom. Another Latina with another trash bucket on wheels clatters after her, an angry clatter from pushing her cart with more force than necessary, as if she too wants to make a statement.

Who tidied up in the execution room—*after*? Trew wonders for the first time. He never lingered long enough to find out. Was it a man or a woman? And how did he, or she, feel about the streaks on the side of the glass through which the prisoner's family looked on—the slobber from kisses, smudges from the press of palms?

It must have been just another one of those messes, just another one of those jobs, minimum wage and outrageous hours, and best not to study too closely what you're trying to erase.

9

Josh: On Dan

Sheree has been tapping with her free hand in a definite pattern—triplets!

"What's this about threesies?" Dan asks, "some kind of magic in threes? Always three wishes in those tales for kiddies—why? Three kinds of people in this country: owners, renters, and rent-skippers . . . Three things that are the curse of Texas—red ants, Johnson grass, and mesquite—can't kill 'em, no matter how hard you try."

He forgot to add the three whistle blasts, rounding up the troops, when our breaks are over . . . Josh is ashamed to recognize his brother spouting off, trying to provoke someone, preferably a girl, doing his damndest to get a conversation going.

And now it's on to more of his bullshit: How we are a great nation because we are a strong nation and a strong nation because we are great.

Dan's staring at Manuel as he says this.

Manuel simply shrugs, water off a duck's back. Like the wetback he undoubtedly is.

What brought this on? Maybe the fact that the Latino has moved from the side panel to the bed, right down there with the best of them.

If Dan's isolated he's done it to himself. He stands alone at the hood, nodding and muttering to his own hands. Then, seizing the cuff with his teeth, he seems to be trying his best to pull out of the left glove without lifting his right hand.

"Too freaking tight," he explains in case anyone's still listening. "Got two fingers in the space for one."

Finally, by biting the fingertips of the glove, he manages to free his left hand. He waves his freed fingers in the air, blows on them.

"Sweat makes them itchy," he announces to the world. As if the others don't know, don't have enough self-control, to keep it to themselves.

If it's not Sheree tapping, or Bev humming, it's Dan's spewing that's driving Josh crazy. *Won't somebody mash the mute button?*

Dan never was over-blessed with intelligence . . . It'll be a neat trick, Josh reflects, to get that glove back on without lifting both hands and disqualifying himself. Josh finds himself smiling at the prospect.

But—*wait*—Josh checks himself, there aren't that many minutes remaining till break. Dan might well make it through the rest of this round with only one glove in contact with the truck, spared having to shift hands again.

Josh is starting to nod but whips back in the nick of time. He can't stare at anything, can't focus, before things start to float. Everyone seems to be under a spell, heads dipping, torsos swaying.

Now Dan's out-and-out flirting with Sheree. Says: "I've got the pepper if you've got the salt . . ." and they're having themselves a giggle-fest. Sheree maybe can't help it, but Josh knows that Dan's doing it just to get on his nerves—

Josh starts humming to tune him out.

10

Dan: On Josh

Josh keeps giving him a side eye. And with that smirk that says: *Can't fool me. I'm on to you—what you're thinking.* Dan does his best to ignore it.

. . . That cocky bastard with his tuttutting put-down laugh! All my life, same story.

But not this time, Dan promises himself. This time, he'll show him!

Can't be long now till break . . .

Dan studies his brother with the keenest interest as he yawns suddenly, taking such a big bite of the air, so wide, so loud that others must hear it—how his jaws crack. It tells Dan that Josh is still holding on, but barely. Won't be long now.

When Dan wins here's what he'll do: he'll sell the truck for that RV he's had his eye on. Go clear across the country.

Then trade in the RV for a Harley, lightly used . . .

But there's *whatsisface—Gib?*—jawing. No let up. Dan sized him up right off the bat, the way he kept wetting his lips with the tip of his tongue. "You look familiar. You know Bill—Bill Everly?" Dan asked. "Sure do," Gib said. So, without another word, Dan knew he'd been in AA and was off the sauce, same as himself.

If Gib's into something else and somehow manages to stand to the finish, he won't get away with it here. It's Dan's understanding that they test the last two remaining. Not a worry for Dan, though. He's clean.

It's Dan's truck. *Meant to be.*

11

About Bev: Second Chances

Nothing is happening and, in hopes of starting something, one of the players is baiting Bev:

"It's in the Bible somewhere, I bet. Or maybe the *Guinness Book of World Records.*"

Still at it . . . It's the one with the nametag "Don"—or "Dan"; Bev can't read it too well from where she's at. This Dan, or Don, or whoever, is standing directly across from her. He reads *her* name perfectly. He keeps saying dumb things like: "Must of hit her funny bone" and "Joke between herself and herself." Laughing or praying, she makes such an easy target.

Half the time she's wearing her headset, feeding her ears, doing her best to mind her own business. But sometimes a hymn tune grabs her so hard that she forgets and doesn't notice that she's singing along. Forgets that others can hear her.

Sooner or later as time wears on, Bev manages to get on *everybody's* nerves. The latest is that whoo-woo-wooing sound she makes. It started with a louder-than-usual exhale, a blowing sound. Then hooting. By now, she sounds like a lovesick coyote. She's got this weird little setup in front of her—like a yard sale shrine, minus the incense and perfumed candles. With each new round she adds on more junk.

"Hey, how about candles?" This Don or Dan can't seem to let it go. "Think God's deciding who gets the truck? Think he gives a fart?"

Bev does her best to ignore it.

"What did God ever do for you?"

"Everything!" Bev is finally provoked enough to reply. "He provides for me. He spreads the table before me. He renews my soul. Without Him, I wouldn't be here, or anywhere, I wouldn't *be* at all . . ."

"And if God happens to forget?" Dan asks. "Or just blinks for a second?"

"No more me, I guess," Bev admits calmly.

One last jab: "So tell me this: An insect with no brain and a hundred legs is born knowing how to walk while a human with two legs and a great brain is born not even knowing how to sit. How come?"

Bev answers, "Ask God!" And tears spark from her eyes.

Bev knows all about faithlessness. How could she not? She's been there, and is still in the thick of it, working as she does as a receptionist in a tattoo-reversal clinic, surrounded by every kind of regret. Business there has never been slack and, human nature being what it is, the names of exes all by themselves were sure to keep it going strong for years to come.

As a trainee the first thing she was taught was: "Never ask the reason. Most will tell you." Turned out, that's exactly how it was. "I'm starting over," one after another. Bev, herself, had come into the clinic as a client with her own regret: a tattoo over her left breast of two hearts joined by a single arrow, circled by a wedding band. And there were words in a banner under the circle:

RAY & BEV 4-EVER

Although Bev liked to say that she couldn't hardly remember why she'd branded herself, she knew it wasn't true. As Ray's name faded she'd even grieved for a while. That passed, but the spot remains tender to this day. Ray had been her honey for six years—she'd cried her eyes out over him—he'd been the whole world for her. The wedding band was a lie, of course: they'd never married. *Thankfully*—how clear she sees this now. The girl working her over sounded sympathetic. Said she'd heard Bev's story many times, the drinking and drugging, being slapped around and made to feel guilty for everything.

Erasing the brand meant starting over. But the mark wouldn't simply dissolve away. The spot was unexpectedly sensitive, the treatment to remove it painful and pricey; it had to be repeated eight times until the particles of color buried in her skin were broken down fine enough to be absorbed, and at the end what she was left with was a faint, shapeless, purple blotch. It looked like a bruise, which in a way it was. So she'd had it tattooed over with a heavy purple cross.

What people wouldn't do to themselves! Bobwire and razor wire in chains were popular—*but why in the world would anyone freely choose to bind ankles and arms with chains?* Teardrops under the eyes were hardest to get rid of, but who needed fake tears when real ones were so easy to come by?

And they'd come in wanting the peace symbol removed; they'd been young when they put it there, everyone had one; now they didn't want to be reminded of those days. It took Bev a while to understand this, to see the true shape of something so familiar and harmless-looking: the peace symbol without peace was really an upside down cross, its arms broken. It was even worse than bobwire and chains.

Business flourished: clients kept flocking, rarely less than ten a day and often more, there was no letup. They had glorified themselves with dancing devils and dragons breathing fire, with snakes twisted and tangled together. Skulls with wings sprouting from their earholes were a favorite, skulls with flames and horns and haloes, crossbones, crown of roses . . . They could, or couldn't, remember why; it didn't matter—everyone coming in had the same wish—to abolish the trace. They all needed to start over. Some had gang logos or prison tattoos that spelled out what they were in for and what they were willing to do. *Try finding a job with one of those . . .* Often they'd been dared—dared to *commit* to something, to anything. One man had the Nike swoosh branded on his back, and then he'd switched over to Reeboks . . .

So, sure, Bev knows all about faithlessness. "The tattoo seemed to make sense at the time," they'd tell her, "the only thing that did." Bev understands, and she believes in second chances . . .

"Go ahead and laugh if you want," Bev says finally when she's mastered her tears, "just blow it off!" She's staring at Gib when she speaks.

Gib has been staring at her, though not laughing outright; he recognizes her as serious competition, and he's been trying to psych her out. He imagines that all her praying might have something to do with her staying power but, beyond that, he still hasn't a clue; he's not at all religious, has no grasp of things biblical, he'd be the first to admit it.

As Gib sees it, the Bible is one wild and crazy book. Few people actually read it. *Think things are crazy nowadays? Take a look, a good look . . . Sex, murder, mayhem, wholesale slaughter, same as now. Maybe worse . . .*

But better not look her way. Let the lady be. Look elsewhere.

She sure gets on his nerves, though—

So . . . think elsewhere.

Nothing is happening and nothing is likely to happen this round and he's thinking of growing a moustache, his left hand rising of its own accord to stroke his upper lip. A risky gesture and a ridiculous one—since he can't feel a thing through the thick cotton of his glove.

12

Manuel: Deciding

Three-forty-four: and fourteen seconds. They are waiting for the dawn of another day. No one speaks. It feels very late.

If this were old times, or if Manuel were with his family waiting through the night, they'd be telling each other stories; but these are later days and strangers surround him so there are no stories. . . . *Why be here?* He tries to remember why he is standing in this place and why these people are standing with him. . . . *Why keep at it?*

But we all want the same prize, he reminds himself. *We're all praying to the big clock, the same clock. For this much, we're in it together.*

Then again, when one of them says, "I'd give my right arm for this truck," Manuel realizes that he would never say, or even think, such a thing, not for a single minute. He knows it's only a way of speaking—*even so . . .*

The whistle for the break coming up should be sounding any minute now. For Manuel, it can't be soon enough. Lots of others have already quit. *(And they were Anglos, so it's no disgrace.)*

Manuel can't wait to return to his family—to Estella, ready to give him a neck rub, and the younger *hermanos* squabbling over who gets to massage his feet. *Not like these other people here, so separate, and so cold.*

Anglos—they're so cold . . .

Why does he think of the *Penitentes* now, in a place like this? He almost never thinks of them; his father does not speak of them.

Maybe it's because his hands are stiff and his knees ache or because he's only partly awake, even though he's standing. Still holding firm, his gloved hands pressed hard against the bed. His eyes are open, but his gaze is fixed on that other place.

It's the *morada* again, the place where *Los Hermanos de Penitentes* once gathered, but empty now, weathered down to bare boards; the roof's cratered, one wall stove-in. It's important to go barefoot, to bear the mark of each pebble and thorn, so Manuel takes off his shoes and carries them. From the *morada* he follows the track of a dry watercourse looking for the place of crucifixion, where he imagines the earth hammered flat from the pounding of feet, but he finds not one footprint, no trace of human presence. Yet someone must of spilled salt on the way, the soles of his feet are burning and why else would the ground gleam so whitely?

Suddenly a path appears. Then vanishes. There is no path—only sky, parched earth, shinnery and scrub—bursts of flowering creosote, clutches of devil's claw, tangles of low-growing mesquite. No sign of the place or the tree he is seeking.

But two tall trees are coming, slowly, towards him. Too far off to tell what kind. They're a pair, walking side by side. A branch from each stretches out to the other.

Look like they're holding hands.

Ahead, too, are many small birds. Farmers call them "wheat birds" since they gather in flocks over fields of grain. And high, high overhead, the kind of birds his *abuelo* called *"viajeros"*— "travelers," they rest on earth so rarely. "They, too, pray for us," his *abuelo* said.

Never owning a truck or car of any kind, the old man once walked over a hundred miles, all the way to a village north of Estancia where a holy man lived. He took along with him only water

and a little food, a rosary and a blanket. When the holy man started to pray over him, he opened the blanket; when the blessing
ended, his *abuelo* rolled up the blanket tight as a candle round its
wick and carried it that way all the way back home. Then he gathered the children and grandchildren and shook out the blessing
over them.

The grandkids, Manuel among them, were too young to understand. They laughed and clapped, batting the air and teasing: "You
catch it?"

"I can't! Can't even see it."

"Me, neither . . ."

Manuel glances down at the truck to which he's clinging. He
knows what his *abuelo* would say if he could see the way they're
fastened, clutching and clinging—to a lifeless thing: *Hold fast to
what you already hold fast to—lose that and you lose everything. This
isn't about the truck.*

He feels so strange, *extraño*. Alone, surrounded by people who
are strangers, he's grown strange to himself. Feels like his heart is
beating outside his body.

A blast from the loudspeaker and the round is called. *At last!*
Manuel is free to peel off his gloves. He does so slowly, deliberately. He lays the pair out flat, marking the place where he's been
standing. His mind is made up, though. He won't be coming back.

"*Tá bien*," he says to no one in particular. *Ya he olvidado. I've
already forgotten.* He parts from the truck cleanly, without regret.
Without a backward glance. He thinks now of the long ride home
in their old truck, the road between here and there stretched out
for mile after mile of pasture and post, with only a windmill, grain
elevator, or gin to mark their passing by. He's surprised to find he's
looking forward to it. Not to be the one driving, of course, that
wouldn't be safe—but riding up front, nodding off now and then.
(He's earned the right to.) Their old Ford Ram gave them more
than two hundred thousand miles before they traded it in for the

Honda pickup they're driving now, so they should be good to go a couple more years with what they've got. It's no beauty but it still gets them where they need to be.

His brothers and sisters will not be pleased; he hopes he hasn't let them down too much. Estella will weep with disappointment— she's only eight. His teenage cousins will miss the excitement and, for their sake, Manuel will agree to hang around *un poco mas*, a little longer, but only to look on. Only till morning. Then they'll climb into the family's old pickup with its dents and scaly patches of rust. Elias will be at the wheel with Manuel beside him, the rest of them piling into the bed, looking to the Anglo world like a bunch of undocumented day laborers. But—*no importa*. They have their papers; the family's been in this country for two generations, after all.

He'd thought he needed the truck to impress his family, wanting to be the Great Man, but knows now he does not need to be. His *abuelo* was—for all of them. Manuel can do no better. Why would he ever want to?

And Manuel feels like a winner already because he's the one who's decided, because he knows who he is. And because he's going home.

13

Five

"Now we go dark for a hundred miles," one of them blurts out suddenly.

It's Number 21—Ken.

He's dreaming out loud, punching the buttons of a cash register he's conjured up out of the air and, to complete the craziness, mouthing little pinging sounds with each jab. He's still in the game since only his right hand is moving; his left remains planted squarely on the hood.

But not for long—

Two minutes later, his left hand falls to his side; his forehead slams metal. When the loudspeaker blurts out the word they all fear, Ken doesn't know he's freaked.

Is he awake or asleep? Half-awake and dreaming? His words make no sense—like his warning to anyone who'll listen not to step through the sheetrock, and to "take the door with you when you go out."

"In dollars we trust," he intones with deep seriousness.

He's been standing next to Gib, and Gib tries to look elsewhere when they come to take his neighbor away. Ken protests that he can't leave—his left hand is fused to the metal. "Superglue," he insists, "works every time." The staffers try to reason with him, "Give it a rest now. Just let go. It's easy—little twist of the wrist is

all it takes . . . Be a good sport. If you make a fuss, you'll spoil it
for everyone. Don't you want people to enjoy themselves?" When
persuasion fails to budge him, Ken has to be yanked and frog-
marched away.

Trew trails after him, recorder in hand; he's hoping for a few
choice lines from this one. The man's mouthy enough, spouting
off a mile a minute. The three halt at the water fountain while Ken
slaps water on his face. The staffers stand back a little to let him
splash. And maybe he'll cool down a bit while he's at it.

"Helluva deal! All you have to do keep your hand on it . . ." And,
turning to Trew, he confides, "I sure could use that truck!"

"You all say that," Trew answers. He's reporting fact, it's simply
a fact; he doesn't intend it as a put-down.

Ken explains how he's in fencing, forty-one years old, still dig-
ging post-holes for another man's outfit. Been dreaming of his
own business—*planning* on it—for his entire adult life. "Can't do it
without my own truck."

He's making his case, sounding perfectly sensible, awake and
aware, when suddenly he breaks off in mid-sentence, leans into
Trew and asks with great solicitude: "You hungry yet?"—his head
so close that his breath clings to Trew's face.

"I'm standing on the hairy edge . . ." he whispers.

When he starts laughing in dry heaves it sounds more like chok-
ing. It isn't good for the others to hear this.

"Better come with us," the staffers tighten their grip. The way
they close in on Ken closes Trew out at the same time, warning
him not to follow—not that he isn't relieved to stand by and allow
the three to pass. Just as well: Ken shuffles along tiredly. Quietly.
Into one of the signing offices—for a debriefing or (Trew has to
assume) to sleep it off. *One has to assume* . . . because how can he,
Trew, follow up? He's only one person and has never learned to bi-
locate. His place is with the contenders still in the running. That's
the main story. Every story is interesting, potentially, but he's been

in the newspaper business long enough to know not to go off on tangents.

There's the squawk of the whistle signaling a new round. Gib takes up the summons: "C'mon, everybody, break's over. Play the game!" he urges. "Let's get it on—get the job done."

Is it a job or a game? . . . And who might "everybody" be? One by one, they've dropped away. With Manuel not coming back and Ken disqualified, only five remain.

They draw together momentarily like the fingers of a fist, then stretch out into the spaces others have left for them, the strong and the lucky, minus the lost.

More room! Gib almost gives a shout. *Subtraction by subtraction, getting there* . . . For an instant, Gib was startled, even a little bit rattled, when Number 21 collapsed as he had—out of the blue. No warning at all. *Could it happen to any one of them? Even to himself?* Gib was so pixilated with joy and dark premonition at yet another player biting the dust, so mixed and marked with *(what was it? . . . doubt? . . . could it be fear?)* he felt sure it must be visible to others, imprinted on his skin, like a rash.

Gib reminds himself how different his own situation is, how cool, calm, and collected he's been all along, how totally alert he is now, how perfectly fitted to the task at hand:

I'm a good shot—I know how to focus.

I'm good at skating—my ankles are strong.

I'm a good swimmer—I know I'm in shape.

I'm good.

14

Clare: Recalculating

Whiplashed into waking, Clare's neck gives a small but audible snap. Her head must've been lolling, jaws gaping—her mouth is so dry. Her last dream, much as she's able to recapture, is all a mishmash: something about a talking dog, a barking child . . .

She'd started out dreaming simply of a woman lying in bed, and a child—*or was it a doll?*—being lifted up to make sure that the woman is able to see it. Clare believes that dreams carry hidden messages, lessons, yet she can't find much meaning in the fragments she manages to salvage after waking. She has no idea who the woman in the bed might be. Of course Clare, herself, can think of nothing she wants more at the moment than to lie down, stretched out to her full length, in bed . . . but she doesn't need a dream to tell her this.

Clare reminds herself that she'll be leaving soon, facing the road again. Soon as she summons up the energy to break away. Just a wee bit longer. But it isn't only exhaustion keeping her; curiosity, even now, is a powerful adhesive.

It's been a while since she caught any glimpse of the lost girl who'd dashed out onto the road or the security guard racing after her on his motorbike. She has to assume the problem's been taken care of.

And to think (she keeps coming back to the image) this was the same girl who'd started her tenth hour putting on makeup, using the reflecting surface of the hood as a mirror . . . Eyeliner, lipstick, and rouge, dabbed on without a fumble using only the one hand! She'd been a picture of calm—or maybe just out of it, maybe a little bored—whatever it was, her coolness had made a lasting impression on Clare.

Thinking it over, Clare finds it hard to believe that she's allowed this contest to eat into her single week of vacation, but, as it must have seemed to everyone else who'd signed on, the deal looked like easy money at the start.

And—something else . . . A feeling she'd been missing out on something in her life. She wanted to be part of whatever it was that everyone else seemed to be part of.

Whatever it was.

Her mom, who's looking after Gabby, loves having any of her grandkids to herself, so that's not a worry. Nor is this a deception, really. Even though no one in the family knows she stopped for this contest, she *is* on vacation; it's not really a lie.

But maybe she'll cut it short. Get back a few days early for some rare relaxed family time. When she'd called earlier in the evening Gabby had refused to come to the phone—Clare had not been prepared for it, the way it stung.

Things were strained between them even before Clare left, and not entirely the child's fault. Clare had begged Sid (her ex, but still, as he reminded her, Gabby's *dad*) not to give in to her pleas for an American Spirit doll. Yes, Clare agreed, the dolls were educational and historical, and politically correct with all shades of brown and beige skin represented, but they were also the source of an endless need for add-ons; another doll, an exact replica in miniature, for the chosen doll, plus a matching wardrobe for all three—the living girl, the chosen doll, and the doll's doll . . . Where would it end? Maybe it didn't matter for people living in L.A., as Sid did now, where money grew on trees.

The doll, a Native American named Enola, wore a beaded and fringed leather dress, as did the soon-to-be-lost and never-named doll's doll. Enola's lace-up moccasins were the next items to disappear, but she could go barefoot—not a problem. The problem was Enola's hair, her beautiful long black braids.

Gabby had promised not to touch the braids, and never for an instant to try and brush them. She'd *promised*. But—*no surprise*—only a few months later, Enola's hair had become a bird's nest of snags and knots.

Clare and Gabby had to make a special trip to Dallas to the American Spirit Doll Center and they'd had to make an appointment at the beauty shop beforehand. There, Enola, "a Kiowa girl growing up in the seventeen hundreds," was placed in a mini styling chair, wrapped in a mini plastic cape—"just like the big girls"—and tended to by a trained beauty operator.

But the beauty operator's verdict was dire: "When the doll's hair gets as knotted as this," she lowered her voice, directing her message to Clare, "I'm afraid all you can do is send her to the hospital."

"And what happens there?" Clare asked.

"Basically? . . . They take off the old head and put on a new one. Only thing they can do."

"A head transplant, then . . ."

"She'll come back better than new, plus a hospital gown and hospital socks and a certificate of good health."

So Clare went ahead with it, forwarding the doll's hospital bill to her ex with all the rest of the paper work. The complete "file": admittance forms, diagnosis (a team of doctors going over the patient head to toe), treatment plan, and discharge papers. Should be arriving any day now. What Clare wouldn't give to see the look on Sid's face when he opened that file!

Right now, with so many of the spectators dozing, and the remaining players standing and nodding, fighting off sleep with little twitches and shakes, all she can do is eavesdrop. There's a wide-awake child two chairs away at the next little family cluster and her mom, speaking too loudly, seems to be reaching the limit of her patience.

"See, what did I tell you? You're not old enough for chewing gum. You always swallow it."

Then the child wants her mom to sing "Ten Little Monkeys." The mom does so, more softly now. Then a small confrontation over "Itsy Bitsy Spider." The mom says "It's 'Eeentsie Weentsie Spider.'" Clare is of the mom's opinion, yet all she can recall with certainty is the spider, the spout, the rain, and the sun. Already forgotten? Yet it wasn't so long ago that she'd catch Gabby singing or reciting the spider song over and over every chance she got.

"I'll give you what for! Don't do that. No, no more eating. Quit wriggling. What's wrong with you? It's too late to be walking around. No, no, no, I said *no!*—don't you ever get tired? Settle down. Better yet, *lay* down. Quit jabbering and try. Here, on my lap, nice and comfy . . .

"Now—doesn't that feel comfy?"

"Sing me again, mommy."

"No more. Shh—shush. See how your daddy's sleeping . . . You don't want to wake him. I know it looks funny to see grownups playing, but it's not a game. It's a contest. It's serious. I know it looks easy, but it's hard. Really hard. Daddy tried his best for us and it wore him out. So he had to stop. But he wants to know who the winner will be. That's why we're stuck here for now. I don't think we're gonna last to the end, though. We'll see. Those people still standing must need the truck real bad—it's no fun."

Gabby would be many hours past bedtime by now . . . She, too, fought sleep; and dreams, what she called "dark pictures," troubled her.

It comes back to Clare like a sudden thaw, a streaming . . . *The joy!* Had she forgotten? Those hours spent leaning over the crib as the baby slept, her thumb wrapped in the clutch of tiny fingers—a reflex, but, even so . . . How content she'd been to sit bedside, simply looking on, matching breath for breath with Gabby . . . And how could she lose those moments when Gabby set out to discover water on her own by poking, pinching and plucking, and the experience of water was given back to Clare as if for the first time? That first freshness could not last, of course. The best days are fading, the future already in sight: American Spirit dolls and the clutter of ever more accessories only the start . . .

Precious time. She must get back.

She'll find a motel—any kind of bed will do—and crash. Give herself time to get back on her feet. She dreads the dislocation, waking lost, not knowing what in the world she's doing in a place like this, but she needs the sleep and will have to face that waking. She won't make a final decision until she's certain she's thinking clearly. Clare's almost sure what her decision will be, though. Once she's freshened up and filled her thermos with coffee she'll hit the road again, in time to be back ahead of schedule. Yes, she's almost sure. She'll surprise Gabby.

Enough of this wasting—

15

Later

It's eerily still. Up front near the staging area, a man sleeps, head flung back, mouth open wide as though singing, singing his heart out—without a sound.

Then—a dog barks, a car door slams.

A boy wakes, shrieking: "But Darth Vader!" Darth Vader has struck off his hand, the one holding his light saber. Now all his power is gone.

Grownups surround the child, assuring him that it's only a dream, a bad dream. "There's no Darth Vader anywhere around here. Nobody wearing a mask. Or black armor. Besides . . . Darth Vader is just something somebody made up. And look—your hand's still attached. Make a fist. See! Your fingers can move."

"But my *light saber!*" the boy wails and will not be comforted until his toy is found.

A few minutes later Sheree's hands shoot up—both hands—as if she's been arrested.

One of the women staffers approaches, places her hand on Sheree's shoulder and calls out "Rules!"

"I'm afraid that's it, Number 9, you just lifted your hands. You know what that means . . .

"I'm so sorry," she adds.

"No, you're not," Sheree is quick to reply. "You're not a bit sorry. You've no idea!" Then: "Who *are* you?"

The woman's manicured nails give a few smart clicks as she taps the plastic badge hanging from her neck.

As if that answers the question.

Then it's back to the quiet. So quiet, you can hear faint pipings from sleepers speaking in their dreams.

As soon as the break is called, and the players have walked off, clapping the blood back into their hands, a man in uniform replaces them on stage. With a soft shammy he strokes the gleaming metal, his back arched like a lover over the hood.

It is hard to see what he sees. There are no marks anywhere on the truck, no scratches. No oily smudges: the thick gloves worn by the contestants absorb sweat, that's the reason they're required to wear them.

All the same, the staffer strokes, caresses, the metal. The surface must be gleaming—mirror-bright.

16

Bowing

The TV monitor is mounted above their heads, pointed at an uncomfortable angle for most of them. No one asks to have it adjusted, though—that isn't it.

They could see themselves on television if they really wanted to, if they weren't more concerned with the digital clock in the lower left-hand corner of the screen, as it emits minutes, seconds, tenths of seconds, and to the scoreboard above it with its tally of how many down, how many standing.

Under the scores there's a continuous crawl of breaking news headlines, weather statistics, livestock and grain market reports: wheat prices, September wheat futures, September soybeans, October cotton, October crude oil, cattle, pork bellies, feed.

If your eyes are blotted with postponed sleep, you might see what Bev sees:

Grain markets come into glory.

What keeps them occupied besides struggling to keep awake?

Bowing. But never leaning or "propping"—disqualifiers they were warned about from the beginning. Bowing is something else. They're all doing it to some degree, as if each were nursing a small candle flame in danger of fluttering out. As if that one candle were the only light in the world.

Just look at Number 11: Bracing himself, thick fingers splayed against the hood, Gib keeps bowing from the waist, taking three short steps forward, three short steps back. It's a way of keeping awake and boosting circulation in his legs, to be sure, but also might look like he's trying to give reverence. And someone stumbling on the scene not knowing what was going on here might well wonder—giving reverence to *what?*

17

Bev: A Few Words

Bev has agreed to say a few words to the reporter at the next break. It won't be an interview. He mustn't call it that.

Here's all she's prepared to comment:

"First thing, let me say that I'm not a bit tired. Not one bit. I'm not seeing or hearing things. The Lord is with me, and I know it. I came for the truck, and I'm not leaving without it. The Lord looks after His own.

"And it's not me alone. I've got a prayer chain from my church here. They're praying up a storm. We're on the winning team, God's team, so how can we lose? No way!"

What Bev will not say is how hard she's struggling from round to round. She struggles to feel what she cannot feel right at this moment: *Remember you've been saved—forgiven, ransomed, redeemed—and not just once, but again and again. Covered by the Blood of the Lamb. Remember to remember that . . .*

Learning to read was the first sign. At first she'd not recognized it for the miracle it was. She was eight at the time, repeating the second grade in a class for dummies and still didn't get it. She'd overheard her teacher saying it was a waste of time and effort, a waste of schoolbooks, "a waste of even a single pencil," trying to make her learn to read and write.

Only eight years old and already she was sick and tired of people always dragging her down, dragging her down, nobody ever raising her up.

When she stared at her lessons the print moved back and forth. Lines flew to pieces; pieces to shreds and tangles. The harder she stared, the less sense it made and the more the letters tore at her.

Then—she still doesn't know *how*—it happened. Seemed like it came to her when she gave up trying. On the other side of the letters lived the meaning. The letters had to fade for the meaning to shine through.

It was different at roller derby where she'd taken to the sport naturally right away and gone on to compete in the all-state for two years in a row. There—she was always plenty quick. And she was quick with music. "Been patting her foot ever since she was born," as her mom liked to say. "And, come to think of it, even before that." Then once she'd found True Vine, her church home, no one watching her there would ever dream of calling her "slow." There, from day one, she'd been the first to clap, first to belt out "hallelujah!" and "amen!"—the first to spring to her feet, arms flung out, singing at the top of her voice:

"Lord, the light of your love is shining . . . Shine on me . . ."

When asked why she's chosen True Vine to be her church home, Bev always answers: "It's very Bible-based." That isn't but half the reason, though. It's the way people at True Vine love on you, if truth be known. Love on everybody if you let them.

She's been redeemed . . . *Yes!* Raised up and anointed. *You bet!* So why doesn't she feel it every moment? Like right this very minute? She looks at the strangers standing around the truck and the strangers watching them, everyone sleep-starved, eyes smudged with unclean schemes, and what she sees is a lost world, herself in it. *Part of it.* She wants to fall to the ground in a wad when she remembers the terrible times, the thick darkness, her fallen self. Time and again— not so long ago—when, brought to her knees by sin, sick with crack or meth and booze, stooped over the toilet and crying for help, the water in the bowl seemed the only font of forgiveness for her. *Paddling her hands in filth, hands stained with filth . . .*

Then she strained to recall her preacher's voice, to recite what he'd taught her:

"The words won't come—yet I will pray. My sins too great—yet I will pray. No use at all—yet I will pray."

No words came, only the twist of tears, yet—somehow—she'd mustered the strength to lift her hands from that unhallowed font and staggered to her feet, determined to start over.

But then only a few weeks after that, how haltingly she'd walked, stumbling, backsliding, struggling to get back on her feet, falling and rising again and again. She knows that her husband (*Lord forgive him*—Bev's trying to, she knows she will eventually, but he has to be sorry first) has been trifling with a younger woman. He's with that woman now, Bev's willing to bet on it. Her brother Bobby, *bless his heart*, is in detox. Back in April he had a run-in with a moving van—a miracle he ever survived with so many bones broken, his truck totaled. He'd suffered a concussion, kept calling it a "confession" (which, in a way, it was). He'd been whooping it up, pie-eyed, loop-legged drunk, as usual. The last thing he recollected was this eighteen-wheeler bearing down on him, headlights aimed straight at him, blazing like the gate lamps of the heavenly portals, blinding with brightness as they searched him through and through. That's to hear him tell it and, if he's lying for Bev's benefit, it isn't the worst of his lies. She takes it as a hopeful sign.

When Bev heard about this contest she knew she'd been summoned, and when she'd walked up to the truck for the first time she'd stretched forth her hand as if in simple obedience to a command. She does not covet the pickup for herself but for Bobby. Winning would prove—be *double* proof (she shouldn't need it but reminders never hurt)—that what she's onto is real, that the Lord *does* look after His flock. And she can see Bobby now when she hands over the keys, his lopsided smile, the gleam of gladness in his eye.

Lord, heal my brother. This pickup is for him.

18

Gib: Qualified

Gib's had a bunch of assembly line jobs. Bored out of his gourd, he'd stuck it out at each of them as long as he could stand it. He figures those experiences should pay off here.

He worked in meatpacking once. Only way to tolerate that was to joke about it like the guys at the gut table calling their job "animal disassembly." Gib was about to rotate to back-splitter, really heavy work, when he knew he'd had enough. All in all, he'd survived it a little over two months. Standing here by the bed of the truck he plans on winning, at what's come to be his station (others may change places but he's made up his mind not to), he keeps thinking back to his meatpacking days. Why? Maybe it's the stiffness in his fingers reminding him of the special steel-mesh gloves he wore at the plant. But in other ways the two situations were completely different: on the kill-floor there was no standing still; nonstop motion instead, hooks rattling, the chain rumbling overhead. Keeping up with the chain—transport empty, transport loaded—having to match it, second for second.

"Men are cheap; cattle cost money," he'd been told the very first day.

Gib had to admit he'd been impressed with how they made use of everything. Nothing was ever wasted: bone went to glue, film, and cattle feed, blood to perfume, ear hair to paint brushes . . .

Standing in blood, the beef kept coming at him at breakneck speed swinging from hooks along the chain—called "cattle" only a minute before, but "meat" now—bodies still warm, still trembling. He had to make the exact same cut over and over—it was called "dropping the tongue"—all the while keeping pace with the chain.

No waste parts, no waste motions.

They'd put up cameras, the time-and-motion men. They had names for how the hand was supposed to move—contact grasp, punch grasp, wrap grasp. They timed the cuts, watching for eyes that drifted. His arm cut, moved apart from him.

He'd grown attached to his knife.

Knife and arm were one, ruled by the chain.

A scene of never-ending motion, the sliding chain, the swinging beef, their hacking arms, blood seeping underfoot . . . and he asks himself again: *Why think of it now when the point here is holding on and not moving—the exact opposite?*

Because in a crazy way—forget the puddles of blood—it's almost the same scene, each moment repeated so exactly it's the same moment, they might as well have been standing still . . .

Good practice, in its way, for what he's doing now.

19

Vince: Nothing Is Happening

"My grandma Alyse was a Blakely, married a Sanborn . . ."

Nothing is happening. Vince is trying to tap into the conversation nearest him while also trying not to be noticed. People have grown used to seeing his equipment lying around and in use, so maybe that's not a problem. They've also quit making his appearance a topic of discussion. Earlier, he'd overheard himself referred to as "that eared beard"; now everyone's grungy and too tired to comment—or care.

He can't help eavesdropping, though. Maybe this latest conversation was never totally a two-way street, but now it's pretty much monologue, with one voice clear and insistent, the other, intermittent and fading, heavily bored. And no wonder—it's totally senseless, a tongue flapping like the clapper of a bell that can't quit jerking. Yet what else can you expect in this no-man's land and godforsaken hour, night on the wane but not yet day? At this hour anything goes and the audience has nothing (really *nothing*) to occupy itself with.

"I love the fishing show best."

"You must like to fish . . ."

"Never touched a rod but it's my favorite show."

Now one of the men is giving out tips for cooking venison. "Soak it in rock salt, then milk. Milk takes away the greasy taste and some of the salt stays . . ."

"Guess you must hunt then."

"Not really."

20

Josh: On Dan, Again

"Joke," Dan says.

"Humor," he adds, since no one has laughed, "is dead." Josh is embarrassed for both of them.

"You two twins?" Number 11 asks.

"But not from the same egg!" the two are quick to chorus.

Josh points to the crest of his gimme cap where the words _TOP GUN_ appear in gold lettering. Neither one can fathom how complete strangers keep finding a resemblance between them.

As fraternal twins, they have nothing in common but a birthday, and as soon as Dan was legally able he'd changed his last name to make that plain. He called himself Dan Streit now—not much different from "Street" to the ear, but placing him at a distance on most alphabetical listings, enough of a difference to make it his own name. That was fine with Josh: if Dan hadn't made the move first, he would have done it himself.

From as far back as Josh can remember, Dan—even though he _is_ the younger, though only by minutes—has been eating up his air . . .

Even though he had a terrible temper and frequent tantrums, everyone thought Dan (called "Danny" back then) was the nicer of the two. He was such a tiny thing to start that the family thought he might not make it. There was reason to be fearful: they'd been three peas in a pod for nine months, with one who'd never breathed literally squeezed to death between them. If that third brother had a name picked out for him, Josh had never heard it.

Since Josh was born first, the family must have thought that Danny, too, had been squeezed. Only Josh was anywhere near full size.

Him being so small, people favored Danny, took his side of things. Always a special treatment. "So cute," they said. "Such a sweetie." He was mute for longer than normal and only began to speak a year after Josh did, and then nothing more than blowback, echoing Josh's words whether he understood them or not. Then, when he did start talking on his own, he said cutesy things, called puddles "cuddles" and "flutterbys" for butterflies.

They'd called him "Little Me Too" when he used to trail after Josh all the time, clinging to him like a shadow, but after Danny got to be Dan, around fourteen or so, the "little" no longer applied. From then on, he was taller and chunkier than Josh. And he was no longer a follower—just the opposite. He was full of himself; the way he rolled his shoulders was a way of speaking.

When Dan gets tense and clenches his jaw you can still see the scar. Or, at least, Josh can make it out far too clearly: he's the one who put it there. Something—Josh can no longer recall what— must have been a powerful aggravation and he'd forced Dan's head into a mirror he'd broken with his first swing. Dan's cheek had to be stitched up; the scar is still visible if you know where to look. It could have been worse, much worse—he might have cut his brother's throat had something not stopped him in time. According to the family, the damage was done, though; that incident shaped the rest of their lives: from then on, their personalities were set in stone.

Josh wants to know: who tipped Dan off to this contest? And why did he follow through in signing on for it? Because Josh had signed—to piss him off? Josh *needs* the truck for his job—he's a handyman—the truck he's driving is a piece of shit. If he doesn't win, he's flat out of luck. Dan does factory work, he has no need of a pickup. Besides—he's already got a four-by-four in mint condition he's customized inside and out that should be enough. And does he really expect to outlast Josh? This contest is all about patience and, as everyone who knows the two of them knows, Dan hasn't a speck of patience, never had.

Right now, Dan's getting ready to raise his voice and order Josh to quit staring, but he'll never manage to spit the words out. Josh can see his throat working, the big empty swallows of air.

Josh reads Dan like an open book, can finish his sentences for him. Nothing too complicated there. Like Dan's habit of staring at the others as if they were coats on a rack: he could care less. He's a manipulator. Been at it for years.

Josh's irritation mounts: a terrible burning itch travels from between his fingers, the palms of his hands, over his neck and shoulders. Now it's salting his scalp. There's no way he can cool this itch. He needs to scratch. And he needs a crotch-adjust, one that stays put.

At last: another break. Josh and Dan dash off for the men's room at the same time. Entering, they move at once to the urinals on opposite walls. They stand with their backs to one another, each staring rigidly at his chosen patch of tile. To their shared dismay, each hears the other plashing in unison.

21

Trew: Nothing Is Happening

"Thought I'd come over and visit with you a couple minutes, seeing it's break time." It's an old man in a John Deere cap. Trew had spotted him milling around earlier, trying without much success to greet people as he passed by. It's way too late for striking up a conversation with most of the audience here, but Trew's on task, eyes wide open; that makes him fair game.

"You're a reporter, right? I'm guessing. Not too big of a guess—since you're the only one taking notes."

After a few words (the man is so eager to talk) Trew asks permission to record their conversation and his visitor shrugs assent: "I guess . . ." Trew hasn't been getting that much in the way of audience reaction and, after all, how often does he find an interviewing opportunity simply dropped his lap like this? Chances are it won't be helpful to his story but you never know; it's something, anyway, to help pass the time and keep Trew from nodding off.

He takes out his pocket recorder, checks it over, aims it: "All set?"

"Go ahead. Shoot."

"So. I'm speaking with Norbert Fix . . . You want to spell that last name for me?"

"F-I-X. Like you do."

"I'm talking to Norbert Fix. You want to tell me why you've come? You family to someone here?"

Fix shakes his head, which the recorder can't see of course, so Trew says "nope" into the mike.

"Friend? Backup?"

He shakes his head once again and, once again, Trew translates for the recorder.

"I'm seventy-nine now—that's a number I don't much like . . . Shouldn't complain, though: I still got all my own teeth. Still squeezing along."

"Retired, I assume. What brings you out here?"

"Just to look. Happened to be driving by."

"Yes, but what's the attraction? Anything special about this?"

Norbert Fix shrugs. "Human nature," he says, "the crazy situations people get themselves into. *Choose* to! See that fella over there blowing on his fingers? His fingers must be burning."

"Itching, at least," Trew amends. He recognizes one of the Street brothers, Josh or Dan; even now he can't tell which is which.

"That's what comes with sticky fingers," says Fix. It never ceases to amaze him "the way people cling to things, then find themselves stuck." And it looks crazier and crazier the older he gets; he's seeing so much clearer now that he's only spectating, retired from the fray. "But, even before," he declares, "I knew enough not to get roped into any lottery, giveaway, super deal, two-for-one, or however they try to flower it up and make it sound pretty. Just watching other people make fools of themselves is enough.

"Bookkeeping was my game."

Retired, and most times glad of it, but—this part not so good— after his wife passed, the kids moved off, scattered to the four winds. "Well, they was grown. It's only natural." He once heard a man who'd lost his wife and kid in a tornado tell a reporter who'd checked up on him months later "I still do life." That's pretty much his own situation. "To prove it I keep moving . . ."

That's why he takes to the road, does a certain amount of visiting kids and grandkids (careful not to overstay), and a certain amount of roaming around by himself.

So happened, he was tooling along the back roads on his way south, fiddling with the radio dial, when he picked up something about this contest.

"Well, sure, there are contests going on all the time. This one sounded different, though . . . Seemed to be all about doing nothing.

"Got more time than money these days," he says, "nothing but time. And it wasn't that big of a detour." Arrived at the sixteenth hour, a few minutes before the break. There were "more than twenty standing at the time. Hard to believe there were once that many—they've been dropping like flies ever since."

He keeps asking himself why they're putting themselves through this. "Look at them! Glued to the metal. For what? Is it worth losing your health? It's just pathetical. Selling the horse to buy the saddle, what it is.

"And say—say you do come in first—what's that damn truck worth? Seventeen . . . eighteen . . . thousand?"

"Top of the line: double cab, four-wheel drive," Trew recites, "and fully loaded—the works."

"The point *being*? So what? What's the point? Look, fully loaded's not the issue. Nobody *needs* fully loaded. Single cab, crew cab, double cab, is it worth it? Let's say that truck's worth thirty thou, thirty-plus. Same deal"—Fix refuses to budge on this. "And afterwards you're crippled up for weeks, maybe months—maybe for good. What's your *health* worth? Seriously. I'm serious."

"Well . . ." Trew waffles.

"That fella who last walked off—he looked pretty steamed. Can't say I blame him. 'Course, he had no front teeth, that takes a bite outta anybody's smile—"

"Now that you mention it . . ." Trew *has* been noticing a gradual shift in mood among the players. They'd started out smiling and greeting one another. A few shook hands across the truck and wished each other luck. The two blacks (both gone long before) exchanged fist bumps.

Along about the second day things changed. "Be nice" was a constant refrain. Later on, there've been frowns, squints, and outright taunts: "Not tired yet? You sure *look* tired!"

And, couple rounds back, when a player announced "Going home—time to get pointed home" right before he quit, only Bev lifted her free hand to wave to him. A few smiled vaguely in his direction, and one of them answered "all ri-ght!" sounding downright cheerful about it.

"How we doing, timewise?" Fix asks suddenly.

Trew taps his watch: "Still break time," he says, "Six away from two. Couple minutes yet."

"Well, anyhoo. . . . I'll be moving on," says Fix. Their interview seems to be winding down. "Selden Hills is where I'm headed. Beautiful country. You never been . . . ?"

Trew shakes his head, "'Fraid not."

"Nice, no kidding. Swing by there sometime." He extends his hand.

"But then you won't be seeing how it turns out here, who the winner is. Why not hang around? The excitement too much for you?"

"Please?"

Trew's been doing his best to rustle up a smile from the man, but Fix regards him with deadly seriousness: "Why? I—I got a feeling about this. Trust me," he shakes his head, "it isn't good . . . A body needs sleep. A mind's gotta rest."

"Well, take it easy." Trew can't think of anything else to say and finds himself echoing the highway sign: "Drive friendly."

Another round, another break. Nothing is happening, and nothing is likely to happen for a while yet. If only he had something to read. . . . There's the *Thrifty Nickel*, but if you're not buying or selling anything, what's the point? There's nothing else but yesterday's paper and nothing so old as yesterday's news. At least the funny papers don't stale—*Dennis the Menace, Beetle*

Bailey, Family Circus, Hagar the Horrible, Blondie, et al., *Zits,* providing fresh poop on a daily basis.

Oh, and the *obits!* They're good for two, three, days. When it comes to names, Trew Reade gets a kick out of finding those as oddball as his own. How about Sam Strayhorn? Ron Breedlove? Not to forget Horace Rodeheaver . . . Trew keeps adding to his collection. He isn't the only one.

He's always liked reading obituaries about people he never knew existed. So he reads about Doyle Newton, Ray Clapper, and Herman Antholz . . . all gone to the Lord yesterday. And how when Ida May Koster went home to the Lord her cancer went away.

Born . . . married . . . preceded in death . . . survived by . . . Apparently, no one notable has died in the area: these are paid-for announcements, phoned in from the funeral home, all pressed to fit the same mold. If last words were uttered, no one has bothered to record them.

His eye drifts to the section below the fold where he learns that Brother Benny Price will speak on "Abiding in the Vine— Entwinement for Life" on Wednesday night at Bethany Baptist Church . . . a stem-winder, no doubt.

This isn't helping with the story he's supposed to be writing . . .

Trew's well aware of what he's up to. Diversionary tactics. Anything, anything at all, to avoid facing the fact that he has no idea what this ordeal means. Is there a meaning to be found here? A story that binds up the fragments—a way to see it whole? Will it occur to him only later, in retrospect?

There are umpteen ways of telling this . . .

There's always the character angle, the play of motive. *Correction: should say: motives plural,* they're not all the same of course. "At least I didn't have to put on a swimsuit to get into *this* contest," one of the early dropouts, a two-hundred-plus pound woman, told him. *No, indeed.* But few of the other contestants have been as forthcoming. The only time he can catch them is during their breaks and, as a rule, they don't take kindly to anyone interrupting their precious few moments of R & R, they're much too wasted.

There's the competitive sports angle: fighters, quitters, losers, the ticking clock. All along he's had a hunch who the winner would be, but different hunches at different times. For the latest: it's the gal, the one who's singing and praying up a storm. She seems happiest, surely the most patient, solid and sturdy enough to outlast the men around her. He could be wrong, though.

Way back, he'd thought it would be the biker dude, who'd come on the scene with a kickass swagger and all the trappings: leather vest on a bare, grizzled, chest, a do-rag round his neck, and one arm sleeved blue to the shoulder with tattoos. He seemed to be pretty well lubricated from the get-go, raising a fuss before changing to the regulation T-shirt, then settling down (more or less) to a position along the bed of the pickup. After that, he'd tapped his way through (the fingers of his free hand and alternating heels) close to the fortieth hour, before he stormed off, spewing words unprintable in a family newspaper.

After that, Trew thought that maybe the Latino would make it to the finish; those people, accustomed as they are to less luxury and comfort, are so much tougher than Anglos. Instead— disappointingly—the boy quit after holding firm for many long hours, giving not the slightest hint beforehand and walking away as if he were simply going for his usual break, peeling off his gloves and leaving them positioned exactly where his hands had been, as if he fully intended to take them up again on the next round.

So, really, Trew has no idea who the winner might turn out to be, and if he thinks of the gal as a strong possibility, maybe it's by way of default, a way of switching off further fruitless speculation.

There are other angles . . .

How about the lure of something for nothing? Might look like it at first, but this isn't "for nothing," though. There's a cost, or there will be; Norbert Fix was right about that.

Trying to engage any of the contestants, Trew's conscious,

overly conscious, of the freedom of his own hands. He finds himself making extra gestures—pipe-fitting motions—when he speaks. He doesn't do this on purpose. It simply happens.

Which reminds Trew: how intensely he's been studying hands, fixated on hands. How (except in the case of Manuel) their hands telegraph defeat, a loosening of the will, well before the actual letting go. There's a pattern to it: a catlike pawing by one hand or the other, then a weak paddling motion, before both hands—as if scorched—leap away from the hood . . .

Why not go on this way? Hang loose for a bit. Simply say what you see . . .

But all he can see most of the time is a bunch of contestants standing, swaying, sweating. Waiting for action.

That's another way to go, though—isn't it?—playing out the question: What makes this contest different? Concentrate on *the surcease from busy-ness, the fact that people aren't running, jumping, or dancing. Holding still is next to being dead to our way of thinking. It's un-American.*

—What now?

"C'm here! Come back!" A mother's shouting breaks the dead-of-night stillness. Trew's on his feet.

Clearly, no one prepared for this particular situation: A child has slipped under the rope that cordons off the staging area. The stage has been deserted since the last break was called and the players rushed off as they always did so as not to waste a second of it.

"All right—just to look," the mother concedes, "just take a peek, don't touch—and come right back."

At the mention of the word "touch," the child stretches out her hand and caresses the door panel as she has seen the grownups do. Her hand leaves streaks from all five fingers and a greasy smudge of palm. "Ma'am! Please!" The dealer's voice rises shrilly through the loudspeakers. "Fetch your child back, please!"

The child is burrowing now, as if seeking darkness, crouching down in the wheel well.

"Ma'am! Grab her—get her out of there!"

"You heard what the man said . . . No, you're not *stuck*!" Kneeling beside the wheel, the mother tries to reason with her daughter:

"You crawl out the same way you crawled in. Just *do* it! Out! This minute!"

No go. Feet flailing, the child must be dragged from the wheel well. She's howling with outrage as an older woman—looks like her granny—takes over and a no-nonsense spanking begins. A staff person enters the ring; he carries a fresh shammy to restore the fender to its pristine shine.

Not quite what you'd call an event but about as much excitement as anyone can expect—or tolerate, really—at this hour. Trew's muzzy with fatigue. *Beyond weary.* Even the blackest coffee has lost its charge. Before, when—*when was it?*—he'd gotten desperate enough to sample the high energy Buster's beverage the dealer was giving out, the drink had done him no favors. Sure, it gave him a buzz, a temporary high, but followed by a slump to match. It couldn't be good for anyone's heart. As far as he's been able to observe, only a few of the players seemed to take to the drink and every one of them has dropped out.

And now? The truck gleams and beckons; the surviving players will soon come together for another round. This could be *it*—the final one—but probably not.

Soon everyone around him, asleep or struggling to keep awake, seems to be nodding. *Here we are,* Trew muses, *together—alone together, each sequestered in a dream.* He stretches his arms, jabs the air overhead; then gives a couple of lateral punches out from his chest. Bringing his hands down, he stares at his spread fingers and, as if struck for the first time, to the webbing between them. Now he's starting to obsess.

There's this trickle of a breeze, then there isn't.

He needs more air. Maybe it would help to get out from under. Exhaust from the Interstate should be dissipated by now.

But once outside Trew finds scant relief. And his vision troubles him. Lamps are bearded; tethered to nothing, they seem to float more than stand; light trails, frays, shivers, borders blur and waver. It's a strange business . . . *Yet not entirely strange . . . not entirely unfamiliar . . .* The moon letting down its rope, the rope dissolving in shimmer, reminds him of moonlight unraveling in water, of the lake, of his summer cottage by the lake where he'd so much rather be.

A stranger, coming upon Trew in his rapt stillness, noting the fixity of his upturned gaze, would first assume that he was stargazing, then (the moon being too bright for stars) might imagine he was praying. But that too would be a stretch: Trew has never considered himself the religious type. And his stillness is only apparent, his thoughts always swirling, never resting.

Yet maybe this much is true: if prayer is in part a way of parsing our desires, maybe, to this extent, Trew *is* praying. He's taking serious stock, at least.

It isn't the first time he's asked himself about hope. He's sixty-one. (Yes, yes, he knows: *Sixty is the new fifty.*) Yet the question persists: *What's left, really?* What might "reasonable hope" amount to in his case? Wouldn't it be a terribly diminished thing? And, when he thinks "hope," why is it that "ambition" comes to mind?

Trew's youthful "hopes" (*ambitions*) had been unreasonable, nothing if not extravagant—he'd nursed them secretly—his own syndicated column, a national scoop, the Pulitzer in due course . . . Hard to believe he'd ever taken these dreams seriously, but he had. He'd never pushed with the required aggressiveness, yet never lacked for ambition either. He lacked something, though, an essential catalyst for ambition—a conviction that his effort, that *any* human effort, made a difference in the scheme of things, that there was such a scheme at all. Maybe the reason he hungers for last words is to tell him otherwise.

For, even now, he hopes to say something about how the nation (the *world*, while he's at it!) is trending, aside from "to hell in a handbasket" by common consent.

A book maybe? If there are still books around by then . . . He'll take his time.

In any case . . . newspapers are on their way out, they simply can't keep pace. Televisual, up-to-the-instant and in-your-face is the way of the future. Trew expects to be retired before paper news becomes entirely obsolete. He'll take early retirement if it comes to that. He can manage.

For, after all, Trew has saved and thought ahead, consistently avoiding extremes, choosing moderation in all things. The safest course: no big wins, no major risks—"minimax" in the words of Matt Stafford, who writes a finance column when he isn't covering the shenanigans (otherwise known as "matters of state") down in Austin. "Minimax," short for "minimizing maximum losses," Stafford explained, is a game and investment strategy that applies to life choices as well.

"It's a way of muddling through—and," he added, "not dishonorable." Stafford didn't disparage him outright, but Trew knew what he thought. *Unadventuresome. Lukewarm.* It's what he thinks himself sometimes.

On the other hand: steady wage-earner since his teens, relieved to be married and settled at twenty-four, tamed and most times glad of it—that isn't, in Stafford's words, "dishonorable."

Once, only once, Trew nearly risked everything. The young woman, an intern, assigned to follow him around, was a breath of fresh air, challenging received wisdom, custom, and courtesy— Trew had all he could do to contain her. He knew that her insistent questioning was part of her effort to impress him. She wasn't especially a looker, but bursting with life and energy. And so young! To a man in his mid-fifties all the young are beautiful. Hard and beautiful. Before the year was out she'd moved on to make a name for herself on a big city paper. Is sure to be married by now.

He filed away those months of temptation and turmoil as "flirtation" years ago, but knows that's not what it was.

Don't go there. That book is closed.

Really, Trew has no one to fault for what he's chosen. No one ever pressured him to accept the tamer work assignment. When it came to choosing whether to flame-out or fade-out, he'd elected the gentler course. His marriage to Heather is as happy as any. He'd opted for ordinary happiness; it has not failed him yet. Both his sons have good jobs, both married with families of their own. His grandkids are still young enough to delight in the world and he in them. If he sometimes speaks of them as "unearned dividends" it's only half-jokingly, for what are they if not pure gift?

No, no regrets.

Thinking ahead to retirement, though, Trew waxes hot and cold. He'll sort it out, or it will sort itself out, when the time comes. One thing to be said for it: there'll be no more deadlines—except for the final one, with years and years, he hopes, of ever so slowly coming undone before that first coronary. Time enough to enjoy whatever peace and quiet he's earned, to make sense of things—or not—at his own pace.

Fishing . . . long walks along the lake . . . moonlight on the water . . .

22

Gib: Smokers

What's happened to that discipline I was so proud of? . . .

None of the other players have joined in, but Gib finally suc-
cumbs to his old craving. *One smoke should do the trick, smooth out
the bumps,* he reasons. He needs some serious calming down.

Is all this worth it? The question is out of bounds. Gib resolved at
the outset never to retreat, never to ask himself; raising the question would mean he's beginning to waver, that his will is weak-
ening.

Of course it's worth it! It's my *truck. Been mine from the start.*
That's as clear to Gib as if the door panels had his name blazoned
across them—

"Need a light?"

Gib nods. Grudgingly. He hadn't realized it showed. He's been
fumbling with his lighter, the flame wobbling, his fingers slippery.
His wrist—just the reverse—is frozen, iron-braced.

He'll smoke only the one, unfiltered as always. *Only this one . . .*

And it does help. One long breath. Then another. He doesn't
waste anything, inhaling his exhale to make it count double.

It's all that coffee and coke, coke and coffee, he's got to have if he
hopes to stay awake that's making him so jittery.

The smokers form a loose circle outside the roofed area of the
dealership. For the most part they stand in silence, content to
breathe deeply. They picture themselves out in the open air; in

reality, they've created their own umbrella of quite visible haze and are huddling under it. Their centerpiece is a spindly ficus tree in an oversize concrete tub. The leaves of the ficus have taken on a grayish tinge, as if they too have been smoking.

"What's your handle?" One of the smokers asks.

Gib's tempted to point silently to his T-shirt which says "11" (he's sweated his nametag off), but he suspects that won't be the end of it. So he says: "Gib."

"What's that the short of? Gilbert?"

Shouldn't have bothered any kind of answer to the first question. Gib pretends he hasn't heard this new one.

"I got problems of my own," the man shrugs, stubbing out his cigarette, and tossing the remains at the ficus as he turns away.

Last puff. Gib's eyes are tearing. He grinds what remains of his cigarette between stiff fingers. A few flakes cling to his lower lip; he uses his tongue, and spits to dislodge them. His fingers still aren't working right—they clump. He fans them out, far as they will go and repeats this maneuver several times. Wrist rotation: ten turns. Now wag the wrist, same number. Now: ten dry swim-strokes, dog paddles for shoulders and arms. He flexes his forearms.

Right side, left side; he stomps six times on each to make sure his feet are working, still able to feel. Add: ten knee bends, ten squats. His knees crunch but it's a relief from the enforced upright.

Now back to the arms. Dog paddle, backstroke, windmill, swimming on dry land, must look pretty crazy. Legs again: *couple more crunches—that's it!* At least he knows the old ball-and-sockets are working, all there, operational. Problem is, it doesn't feel like the machinery belongs to him.

Gotta get my shit together . . .

So it's back to his chair for his gloves and a few quick glugs of coke and coffee. He's ready. *Truly.* Ready as he'll ever be.

Here comes the blast of the public address system firing up. Then the voice of the dealer: "Clock's ticking. Back to your places if you want to be counted. Sorry to report: your break, boys and girls, is over." He's grinning into the mike as he says this, that's how sorry.

But aren't they all, secretly or openly, wanting to get this show on the road, wanting for it to be over? And at the same time dreading it, wondering *who'll be out next? Will it be me?*

23

Dan: Chairs

Still standing—

Going nowhere in this crazy standstill race. They're down to four, all in the back now, positioned around the bed. The area could be comfortably divided into quadrants, except for the fact that Josh and Dan seem to be preserving the distance for three, as if some invisible person stands between them.

Dan makes a point of not looking in his brother's direction:

Head up, eyes front. Feet planted on concrete, hands planted on metal... Steady ahead, not to be blown away.

Dan warns himself: *Don't even think of sitting down* . . . At once he is mobbed by images of chairs, a parade. They come in every shape and size, more kinds than he'd ever known he'd noticed: benches and barstools . . . straight-back . . . ladderback . . . basket weave . . . butterfly . . . bucket chair . . . What they use to call "easy chairs" . . . Rockers, recliners, La-ZBoys . . .

La-ZBoy! . . . Right now he could be tempted to trade in this truck for one of those. *Gotta keep the truck, only the truck, in focus—*

It's three in the morning, the audience down by more than half and most of them nodding off, but not one of the four surviving players is budging.

24

Gladys: Three in the Morning

Number 7, the girl he captured bolting for the freeway, has been safely corralled into one of the small side offices used for finalizing contracts. She's been sleeping in an upright position, occupying two chairs, the second chair to prop up her swollen feet. *Asleep or faking it?* He still can't tell for sure.

Fidgeting in his upholstered chair, the security officer watches the girl closely while his hand moves over the legal pad in front of him. He's been covering the page with clock faces, maybe because he's stuck on thinking of time—time passing or stalling, mostly stalling. When he makes an effort to imagine something else, what comes is nothing but up-and-down strokes like the bars of a cage. He doesn't trust the girl for a minute.

He can't forget how calm and collected she seemed at the start. Watching her standing there, using the hood as a mirror, dabbing on makeup with only the one hand, he thought she'd outlast most of the others and might even have a decent shot at winning.

At the moment she gives every *appearance* of sleeping, a good imitation, if not the real thing. She can't fake it forever, though. He's prepared to wait, however long it takes. He's gone over her paperwork (it's evident no one else has) and is inclined to doubt everything about her. All the blanks on the registration form are filled in but, except for the name "Gladys" (itself doubtful), the writing is mostly illegible. The numbers look bogus, they're too consistent, and the handwriting's squashed, as if ashamed of itself.

How'd she ever pass?

Why was she ever allowed to enter the lineup without a valid I.D.? Who approved this? His hunch is that some young man on the staff liked her looks: she'd batted her eyelashes and he sneaked her in at the last minute to fill an empty space left by someone who failed to show. Instead of a driver's license, she'd handed over a Walmart gift card made out to one Gladys Weld. She doesn't look like a Gladys, the name's too old fashioned. The gift card could have been for anyone; she might've found it dropped on the ground or tossed by mistake into a dumpster. Or she might of stolen it, he wouldn't put it past her. He's almost sure that's the story, something along those lines.

She's a looker, that's for sure.

When he asked her to empty her pockets, all that she could come up with was small change, half a comb, tube of lipstick, and such. Then a key to someplace or other—she claims not to remember where—so he must try and find out. To keep himself awake he keeps his pen moving. Ladders and wheels. Spokes and stars. An eye, all pupil, with spiky lashes like the rays of the sun. Didn't know he had it in him.

A week from morning, feels like . . . Gladys takes in the room through her lashes, one slit eye at a time. How much longer can she keep on pretending?

Still, it's not like she's completely faking it; she isn't fully awake, not really. Feels like she hasn't been really awake in a long time, needing the smack of pavement on foot-soles for that. Right after she'd quit the truck she tried clapping her hands to get the feeling back but it didn't work. This went beyond numbness: her hands didn't seem to belong to her anymore. She's never been frostbit, but imagines this is how the first stirrings of recovery would feel, a tingling, faint, far away. She had to bite the tips of her fingers one by one to be certain the fingers were her own.

Little by little, some things are coming clear.

A near-empty gumball machine next to a watercooler. Standing in a smokers' huddle, bumming a cigarette off of somebody she didn't know. People scattering at the blast of a loudspeaker . . .

A thought, the echo of a thought: *Not all promises can be kept . . .*

And her name—how could she forget *that*?—is Jenelle. With three *e*'s, No resemblance to "Gladys."

She remembers people clinging to, what was it? Lifeboat? Raft—people clinging to a raft, what they thought was a lifeboat, and she too was clinging. *"Hardbody,"* they called it, but it was flimsy as water. As air. A man's voice: "I think she's cashing out." She was going down. If she held on any longer she knew the raft would sink and she with it—

She bolts upright with a question: "Did I say anything?"

"Not that I noticed." The guard tosses his pen aside. He leans over the desk: "Wanna tell me why you've been going by a fake name?"

"So silly of me." She tries her smile. She's not sure. More of a question to her mind is: *why that particular name—why Gladys?* Her memory's as porous as lace . . .

You don't trust me, she thinks, *and I don't trust you.*

"Let me get this straight," says the guard. The girl's head is lifted back, eyes half-shut: looks convincing, like she's trying to remember—working at it, at least. Staring at the smooth white stalk of her neck, he thinks: *it's too perfect, too white.* He wants to sink his teeth into that skin, leave a signature.

"Changed your mind? You don't think your name is Gladys?"

She opens her eyes and stares back at him: at his security badge; at the lamp—too bright—then cuts her eyes away, not saying.

He keeps twisting his fingers, knotting and unknotting them.

He'd be willing to bet now that the gift card this so-called

Gladys presented as an I.D. was stolen. Definitely. She definitely looks like someone who'd know how, someone who'd be cashiering at one of those big box bargain stores like Walmart or Target, a walk-in hire, easy come easy go. And, chances were, it wasn't the first time she'd pulled a trick like this.

When she lifts the hem of her shirt to wipe her nose, he catches sight of her midriff, the skin there as white as her neck. One thing he knows: She hasn't been laying out on the sand, *lazing* the summer away out on a beach somewhere, he'll credit her with that much.

This isn't the craziest contest he's ever covered, though it's got to be the most wearing. That chainsaw tournament in Arkansas years ago would have to come top of his list for crazy. He'd picked out the winner at first sight—the one calling himself the "Wild Mountain Man" who came from logging country up north and who sculpted "the world's fastest chair." Took all of twenty-eight seconds. Then he etched a man's initials on the buckle of a belt with the man inside it.

Not to forget that kissing marathon where even the winning couple had to admit that their lips had grown numb; if they'd been in love before, they couldn't stand each other by the time the contest was over . . . Couldn't look each other in the face. They divvied up the cash prize but didn't bother to scrap over the trophy cup, never touched it, they were in such a hurry to split.

He's seen a thing or two in his time.

"Voted off the island . . ." Gladys says, thinking aloud. But, she reminds herself, it wasn't an island, it was a raft, and she wasn't voted off, she chose to let go because the raft was sinking. They were all clutching and clinging. She knew it would never hold them up.

Then she was sinking . . .

"What's a girlie girl like you want a big truck like that for, anyway?" the guard asks suddenly.

It isn't a real question, just another one of those remarks, so she lets it pass.

And anyway it was never about the truck, really. What then? Something owed her. *There had to be something to even things out . . .*

Something taken, something owed.

Things are coming back to her. Threads . . . Her memory's as porous as lace.

Lace . . .

The way she's dressed now it's hard to believe that only weeks ago she was standing at the dressmaker's, getting herself pinned up in a long white gown. *A dream of a gown . . .* the bodice and sleeves all lace. She sees the gown in her mind's eye clear as can be, but can't recapture a single image of herself trying it on, of actually slipping her arms into the sleeves, buttoning the tiny buttons and posing for that final fitting. All she can see is the glare of mirrors reflecting walls.

Oh, and the dressmaker standing there, not speaking, pins held between her teeth—

It occurs to her only now: the dressmaker's name was Gladys—

*Then, another thing—the afternoon of the wedding—it's coming back in a flutter—now it comes!—*a confetti of fine detail . . . A voice, not hers, calling out, "Half past!"

She recalls telling herself: *Must be traffic,* then: *He's only a little late . . .*

The others, settling into pews, are chattering softly. Something chimes: it's the wedding planner's cell phone, buried in the bottom of her purse. The phone cannot be retrieved quickly enough. The tune from "Here comes the bride" is the ringtone. It cannot be stopped. The priest, gone inside, is busy housekeeping, or counting money, or whatever priests do with themselves in private. Jenelle has paced the aisle and now stands watch at the outer door, peering up and down the street. Cars pass but not the one she's looking for. She stands and waits, alone. She is not joined to anything...

But here the guard seems to be winking at her. Or maybe *she's* the one doing it. She's been blinking hard. His head's tilted like he's getting ready to ask a question.

Ignore him.

... She's standing watch at the outer door of the church, cars come and go, the afternoon shines, the forecast fair for the coming days. Already, she knows: *It will never be better than this,* when the best man shuffles in and it isn't.

He's bringing a note, an explanation: *Not all promises can be kept.*

The rat.

It's over: the wedding planner gathers her candle-stands and bridal arch, packs up the flower girls' baskets. The freeze-dried rose petals meant for the baskets are already wilted and have to be carried straight to the trash.

This isn't the first time a bridegroom has gone AWOL on her, the planner explains, predicting that she'll be called back before the year is out: same bride ("that's you, Jenelle, yes, you!") with one groom or another. The priest tries to console her with "Better now than later on." The bridesmaids hang around and hang around, insisting on their all eating together regardless, after they cancel the restaurant dinner. It's Chinese takeout so at least she'd have something in the fridge when she feels hungry again. "Which you will," they assure her. None of them have much of an appetite right then. What conversation there is recalls happier times. Jenelle, herself, can neither speak nor eat. By then she feels nothing much one way or another; she seems to have entered a deep freeze.

Afterwards—moving to a new place, clearing out the memories, avoiding old friends, doing her best to leave the past behind...

She intends to slip away as soon as she gets the chance. She wants to step far, far out into the night, and soak up darkness. Only this one security person standing in her way—

He's starting to slump, nodding as if consenting to something, then catching himself, snapping back sharply, denying it. *Yes, no, yes . . . almost . . .*

Won't be long now.

25

Trew: Voices, Roving

Night. Interminable night.

Nothing is happening on the main stage. Just the same four players nodding and swaying. They move like seaweed streaming in a deep current. Most of the audience is napping but there are pockets of wakefulness here and there.

Trew, pacing round and round the perimeter of the showroom in an effort to keep awake, catches two young men arguing—it's one way of fighting off sleep. They seem to be at the tail end of things, though, or maybe there never was that much at stake. The one stretched out in his deck chair, fingers draped over his eyes, doesn't look long for this world; the other, leaning forward, seems to be going strong. He's speaking much too loudly and glancing around in hopes possibly of drawing others into their discussion, but no one else is biting. Still, he keeps hammering away:

"Life has no meaning. Your asking 'What's the meaning of life?' has no meaning. Words have meanings—words attaching to other words, that's all. It's like somebody asking 'What's the *meaning* of the chair you're sitting on?' The question makes no sense. Wrong context, different language—a category mistake. See what I mean?"

"I . . . guess."

"Whad'ya mean by '*guess*'?"

The man in the deck chair lets loose a sigh of profound weariness: "If you say so," he says, his voice fading. There's more energy in the group gathered near the smokers' corner, where people are placing bets. They stand in a ragged huddle, arguing about luck and willpower, whether it's one or the other or both that the winner needs. Whether there's such a thing as fate. They were placing bets on the contestants earlier—singles mainly, nothing larger than fives—now they've upped the stakes. Ten's the limit, though. Most of the money is on willpower with bets evenly divided between the two brothers. Those who own up to thinking that Bev is the one who's going to outlast the competition are only praying for her, they don't do bets.

Trew moves on, taking notes on anything and everything, hoping for inspiration.

There's this latest page of jottings, a ragbag of jokes and teases. Calling the truck "the Going-Nowhere boat," for instance. One of the players dubbed it the "mother ship." When the whistle blew for a new round, he called out "Okay everybody—it's back onto the mother ship!" Who was it said this? Ken? Sounds like Ken. Long gone now.

And the teases: an innocently-worded question like "How you doing?" comes with a nasty barb depending on how it is said and who's saying it.

Right now it's Gib fixing on Bev: "Bet you're tired. You look tired."

"Doing just fine! And yourself?"

"Livin' good!" Gib shoots back with a big smile.

With Gib and Josh ever at her, Bev must be perfectly aware of what they're up to. It's obvious: Not at all happy that she's outlasted so many of the men, they're doing their best to psych her out.

A child sips from the snout of his water pistol. It's late, much too late for any kid to be up and about.

Now there's a panhandler, a woman with swirling, startling red hair and eyes that hop, approaching Trew. She's been working the crowd—with no takers that he's noticed so far. She's not done trying, though. Anyone with eyes open seems to be fair game. There's no dodging her and, before long, she's on to Trew, shoving a printed card in his face. Looks like what used to be known as a "calling card," though it's soiled from much handling, and makes a poor introduction to the presenter.

The language is quaintly old-fashioned:

> *LADIES AND GENTLEMEN!*
> *I am deaf & dumb.*
> *I am selling this card to see my way through.*

But we're all trying to see our way through, Trew says to himself. *We're all just muddling through.* The message goes on to promise many blessings—of health, long years, and prosperity—to the giver.

He's convinced it's a scam. The deaf are still with us, but is there any excuse for muteness nowadays? Trew thinks not and is about to hand the card back when the woman snatches it from him with a harsh braying cry and rushes away—evaporates into thin air. There's no other way to describe it.

Trew wonders, flickeringly, where all the disqualified players have gone. They, too, seem to have vanished.

Is this what they used to call the "witching hour"?

26

Gladys/Jenelle: Away

Jenelle, aka Gladys, waits it out, studying her captor through half-closed lids—

—Until he slumps and buries his face in the nest of his folded arms.

Ever so slowly, she starts to lower her feet to the ground, suspending before touching down, testing. No response. *But wait. Could be a trick.* She stares at the hands in her lap.

Here are two hands—a giver, a taker...

Air! She needs air!

As the man's breathing steadies to a drone, Jenelle rises and softly paddles over to the desk. She finds a pen and memo pad at the ready. Her hand is quivering as she does her best to print:

GONE TO THE LADIES

Then, for good measure, she pauses, leans over his slumbering head (noting the comb-over, the few sad gray hairs carefully pasted to his scalp), and whispers:

"Be back in a jiff." Fearful that even the click of the latch might wake him, she leaves the door ajar.

Free! Out in the open air—she's wide awake now, aware of her heart yammering in her throat. But she moves slowly at first. Her feet as well as her hands have gone queer on her; her fingers are stiff as prongs, the soles of her feet rubbery.

Anyone following?

Not a soul.

She's on her way—*where?*

She hasn't the thinnest thread of direction to start. Just: *away—anywhere—to get away.* She passes a sign GOODBUY something or other, too impatient to be on her way to pause and make out what it's an advertisement for.

She wishes she had a photo of herself standing for that final fitting to prove it was ever real . . .

She can recall the ad she placed in the Classifieds, at least the heading, four words—each letter—razor-sharp:

WEDDING DRESS NEVER WORN

. . . A dream of a gown. Lace, dotted with? Pink . . . Tiny little pink roses—what were they called? The words "blister roses" come to mind, but that can't be right. *Rosettes? Anyway . . . sleeves with long wrists and tiny embroidered buttons, fake buttons, made to look like rosebuds, hiding the snaps underneath.*

She loved the neckline . . . *the scalloped neck, fitted bodice, bustle. and train. And the veil.* "Illusion veil," they called it. *They got that right.*

It fetched a decent price after all. Fraction of what she'd paid for it, of course . . .

The ground furrows like sand under her feet. Her steps are still uneven, unsure, her fingers trailing. There are no handholds.

Crossing the city lot where the school buses are parked, things change. Now she's slapping along in her noisy flip-flops, moving with a sense of release, amazed that she's able to walk at all, marveling at the fluency, after being cooped up for so long. Still—she reminds herself to be careful, not to lose sight of the highway running parallel and close alongside.

Listen!

It seems to be nothing more than the rustling of a light breeze at first.

Gradually, Jenelle has become aware of an echoing sound, a faint *shluf . . . shluff*, then the harsh scrub of rubber on asphalt. Something hissing. She cries out in fright—the cry escapes her. But—*it's crazy!*—hasn't she been expecting this, known all along it would come?

Still racing, she turns her head, enough to make out a moving blot, a car without lights slowly gaining on her, gaining but teasing, not yet closing the distance.

She isn't dreaming—for suddenly it's beside her, a man's voice crooning:

"Hey, girl!"

Through the open window, a white hand beckons—*a white man—*

"Hey . . ."

Don't say a word.

She clenches her toes and takes off—fast as flip-flops can— slapping and scraping across the deserted parking lot, zigzagging right and left, forcing him to twist and turn, hoping to keep him off balance.

Lights ahead—the blazing lights of an all-night Toot'n Totum. *Almost there!* She stumbles the last steps. Over the threshold—

She's in!

With a shriek of brakes, her stalker veers. Vanishes, sucked back into darkness.

Jenelle's breath comes hard, heart pounding, eyes stung with tears, all alive now, alive and awake, refreshed by fear.

Through fear to feel.

Then the moment passes.

27

Dan on Josh: Road Rage

. . . Anybody here check his driving record? Dan doubts it. All those so-called minor infractions? Then ask some hard questions of his insurance agent who's got a crush on Josh and bends over backwards to get claims erased from the record or settled in his favor. Had the contest officials ever bothered to look into it, they'd realize that he wasn't exactly a poster boy for new car sales.

Josh knows all the rules and loves reciting them: following too closely is an infraction, failure to signal you're stopping—an infraction . . . *Vehicular homicide—if he's to be believed—a misdemeanor!* As far as Dan knows Josh hasn't tested that one yet. *Only a matter of time—*

And, if anything, Josh sober is worse than Josh drunk. He was only tailgating, cussing, flicking a finger to start with—not to forget all the paint he rubbed off of cars parked in lots—nothing at all compared to the lane-cutting, shadowing, slamming, and deliberate fender-bending after what he likes to call his "cure."

Anything, anything at all, is likely to set him off: a bumper sticker, a horn, a woman angling for the same parking spot.

He once crushed a *MOWERS AHEAD* sign because he decided it would slow him down. *Hard to believe! Isn't there a law—damage to city property or public endangerment or something?*

So, say Josh wins . . . This beauty will be wrecked within the month, Dan's willing to bet.

They should of checked . . .

How did they decide who was eligible? Was it simply anyone and everyone with a driver's license whose name came up in a drawing of lots?

You had to wonder.

28

Bev: Singing

Seems like people are winking at her. But isn't it more likely, Bev reminds herself, that they're only blinking—blinking hard—doing their best, as she is, to keep awake?

Morning soon on its way, though you'd never know it by looking. The darkness is unrelieved. *Yet why not start the new day singing?*

She can't help swaying as she sings: "On Christ, the solid rock I stand . . ."

Since she's wearing headphones she can't hear herself full volume; she forgets that others can.

". . . All other ground is shifting sand . . . is shifting sand . . ."

Josh speaks for the rest of them standing around the bed when he asks her to pipe down. It's not at all clear that she hears what he's saying.

Bev lifts her eyes to the top of the tent as though to the heavenly hosts and proclaims: "To God be the glory! I'll stand for Him and He'll stand for me."

"Good, that's settled, then," Josh says. "Give her a harp and wings, already!" and he turns to Gib for support. Gib only shrugs. He doesn't waste energy.

Let them laugh . . . Bev welcomes their scorn. As the One she follows was scorned.

"Glo-ry!" she belts out, undeterred. "Praise the Lord! I praise Him and give Him the glory! And I'd say that atop the tallest building in the world."

"Pul—ese, you're giving me a headache. I'm asking nice now," Josh says, "I won't next time."

Bev continues, but in a bare whisper now:

Lord, the light of Your love is shining . . .
Shine on me,
Shine on me . . .

29

Trew: Dark, Speaking

He's eating his own hand, starting with the thumb; the meat is tender but has no flavor. There's a phone ringing: it's his wife. She's at their summer cottage by the lake. She tells him his father has just called from his mission in space; he wants Trew to call back right away. Trew's standing outside the cottage smoking. He's leaning against a tree, smoke extruding from his nostrils in slow curling streams. Someone breathes in his ear. A voice-over: "This is real, not reality television . . ."

He knows it's only a dream since he quit smoking years ago. And his dad died a few days before Trew's twelfth birthday. His dying (a *fact,* no doubt about it to his adult mind) is etched forever in his memory because it happened so suddenly he couldn't believe his dad was really dead. The body was covered head to toe when it came back from the operating room and Trew had been spirited away at the approach of the returning gurney, so he couldn't be sure it was his father's body humped under that sheet. Because he'd only gone into the hospital for what they called "minor elective surgery," and because (Trew keeps coming back to this) the last words his father had spoken would never do as words of farewell, Trew was sure he'd come back and explain. *Somehow explain, say something more.* His dad would never quit and say nothing. It wasn't like him, so he couldn't be dead—that was Trew's thinking back then, still a child. His mother had to drag him to the funer-

al home before the cremation and ask that the body be taken out
of refrigeration before Trew was convinced that there would be
nothing more.

Trew never questioned the fact after that. The body was swad-
dled to its shoulders in clear plastic. Only the face remained familiar,
but with an expression of puzzlement—or was it astonishment?—
in the lift of the eyebrows. His father's eyes were shut but he was
still wearing his glasses.

"Could you take them?" his mom asked. "I can't."

When he lifted the glasses from where they were hooked over
his father's ears, trying to touch only the plastic stems, his hand ac-
cidentally brushed skin. Trew's fingertips burned with the cold . . .

It's gotten actually chilly outside.

Back at the staging area, the contestants are still standing in place,
still nodding and swaying, although the nods seem to be lowering
with each pass. Moment by moment it's getting harder—they're
holding on for dear life now. But until one of them crumples, nothing's likely to change.

"Little bit longer," someone in the audience calls out. "It's got
to end soon."

No help for it in the meantime but continue to wait. Reclaiming
the folding chair he brought along, Trew leans back and, himself,
folds.

. . . It's a lawn party, voices gabbling, he's mingling poolside
with people he doesn't know. The theme music from *Happy Feet* is
playing softly; the sound of water lapping grows louder, insistent.
The ground shifts, there's nothing firm under his feet; paddling fu-
riously to stay in place, he's swept along by the muddy, swollen,
water, with coats and dresses, cabinets, shoes, sofas, trees, and an-
imals swirling past. Something—some terrified creature, cat-sized
with tiny claws, scrambles onto his back, trying to ride him to safe-
ty, as Trew himself grapples for handholds, snatching at anything
rooted or solid, tree trunk, wreck of a car or pickup, a hard body of

any kind. *Nothing stays, the clinging creature plunges*—when the subtitles come on, Trew cannot read them.

He wakes, hands clutching nothing but air—

It's strange . . . being in the dream and at the same time outside it, both watcher and watched. He's dreamed with captions before, but only when things got really scary, out of control, one of those mind tricks, he suspects, keeping him safely distanced from deep trouble. Maybe that's it: a way of distancing, while still keeping connected . . . Still—what's the use of subtitles in an alphabet you can't read?

In any case . . . Trew reminds himself that the only danger facing him at present is the all too real possibility of falling back to sleep, missing a critical moment—he needs to be on maximum alert as they enter the final rounds.

He hears quite distinctly someone close by saying "It's been decided." But when he looks up, he sees the same four remaining players standing as they were. If anything, they seem more desperately glued to the metal than before, like barnacles stuck to a rock—or, no, more like shipwreck survivors clinging to a raft, dipping and swaying but holding fast as they meet each oncoming wave.

Nothing's been decided, nothing has changed.

But then—wait a minute—the Street brothers are shouting—

30

Dust-Up

Somebody blowing a gasket—

Unclear whether it's simply the urge to make things happen rather than wait for events to declare themselves. One of the brothers, the taller—or the one who *looks* taller because he's wearing a cap, the cap that says <u>TOP GUN</u>—is fairly prancing with rage. And sputtering—"Everybody sleeping? You people blind?"—insisting that his brother Dan "flicked" him, lifting one hand to give him the finger, then both hands to scratch his nose.

Dan smirks: "So how come nobody else saw it? Maybe you been dreaming?"

"Nobody was looking, dammit! Everybody blinked. And you fucking well know what you did!" Josh fumes under his breath, well aware that a single obscene word if spoken aloud would have him disqualified on the spot.

The judges shrug. One of them speaks: "Take it easy. Better ease up, you two. That means both of you. If nobody saw it, it never happened. That clear?"

Trew wonders: How on earth could the judges fail to notice an incident like that (if, in fact, it happened)? But maybe it was a mirage—no one knows for sure. Everyone seems to be slipping some. Trew, fighting sleep every minute, can't afford to let down his guard. Nor can the cameraman—Vince, who's suddenly snapped to attention: "What'd did I miss?" he wants to know.

31

Bev: Glory!

Seems like the canvas top which covers them is being lifted for inspection and Jesus is smiling down at her, at *her*—Bev especially. She doesn't really see the truck anymore—only *Him*, his face like the sun, basking in glory.

"Jesus has the whole world whipped! You bet! Amen!" Bev shouts out and, without pausing for breath, she's off again singing much too loudly. About a bright land beyond the sun promised to all the faithful, and a house ready and waiting for her, gold on the outside, silver inside.

"Sounds pretty chilly to me," Dan objects, "I wouldn't want to live in metal of any kind, come winter." And suddenly Bev's speeding up, racing along on all sixteen cylinders, still carrying on about that bright land yonder, too busy to reply that of course there'll be no more winters there. Part of her knows it's too fast.

Then Dan sings out "Yonder!" And again "Y-ah-ahn-der!" with a sort of yodel, just a tickle of a tease, no real harm intended.

Bev answers with a "Thank you, Jesus!" and "Praise Him!"

She calls out "Glo-ry!" and "Amen!" again, letting loose such a yelp it's clear she's forgotten where she's at. But how can she help it, how can she stand there froze up like a statue when she's on the winning team, on the home stretch, and the Lord is on her side?

And then—there's a clutch in her throat—she's getting ahead of herself!—her hands give a glove-muffled clap and her arms, banners of the Spirit, fling high to proclaim the victory sure to come.

"Glory!"

High and wide, for all the world to see.

"All to Jesus . . . I surrender . . ." Fainter now. She mouths the words brokenly—only now realizing what they've cost her.

She's out.

A clear judgment this time. Nobody questions it, leastways Bev herself. Someone in the audience calls out appreciatively, "You came so close—" Strange consolation!

Two attendants step forward to assist Bev. One gathers what he calls her "tack" from the hood. With earbuds trailing, clutching her tape player which is still running, Bev staggers, stumbles, falls to her knees—

Neither handhold nor foothold . . . but on her knees . . . *the only steady place.* The only place for her.

But then she turns and sees B. J., Lena, and Misty from the True Vine prayer chain rushing her way. They stoop to gather her, and Sammie joins them to come raise her up. Together, they steer Bev forward, easing her down into a waiting chair.

Bev's sobbing is as much from sheer exhaustion as from loss; everyone realizes that. No help for it except to massage her shoulders and sing for her. It's "Worthy Is the Lamb," one of her favorites.

Then they shift to something calmer. Should be soothing:

> It is well with my soul . . .
> it is well, it is well with my soul.
> Even so, it is well with my soul.

Bev, weeping through it all, is not even trying to mouth the words.

Trew has followed the crowd and stands aside waiting for a chance to have a few words with Bev. It doesn't look like she'll feel up to it anytime soon.

Another onlooker standing next to him explains: "Her heart's broke."

"Yes." Trew is not about to dispute it.

"No two ways about it."

"Yes, I can see that," Trew agrees. Problem is: Trew can only afford to hang around a minute or two; then, if Bev's still not up to talking, he'll have to return to the staging area and get back on track. The game won't wait.

32

Three

So that's another one out—they're down to the wire now. The three remaining stand stiffly upright as if tied to stakes, they don't dare to be seen sagging.

There'll be a time-out right before the upcoming break for whoever survives this round. The almost-winners will be escorted to the men's room and asked to piss into plastic cups.

And they'll be watched closely as they do this to prevent any "funny business."

Betting is keener now, as they near the end; they're up to fifteen, twenty dollars a throw. Trew hasn't taken a survey but, from the random little he's observed, the bets seem to be evenly divided among the three. It stands to reason. The three remaining contestants seem to be equally firm, equally determined.

But there is one thing Trew's noticed, a small detail of questionable importance. Gib—Number 11—is standing with his feet spaced wide apart. This gives him the advantage of a wide base and added stability, less potential for wobble. Suggests the kind of minute calculation that might well mark a winner.

Even so, Trew's not putting any money down. He has a profession to uphold. Besides which, he has a hunch (no idea where it comes from) that the contest is going to implode, everyone letting go, giving up, and finally by default, the judges being forced to draw lots to end it.

33

Jenelle: Release

It's her breathlessness and guilty glancing around that captures the attention of the cashier at the all-night Toot'n Totum. That— and the godforsaken hour. Only certain kinds of women can be found out on the street at this time of night. Doesn't look like she's one of them, but you never can tell.

She stands and stares at the first display she's come across, magazines she doesn't bother to pick up. Her behavior is a bit strange, but seems harmless enough, so he ventures: "Hot enough for you?"

He doesn't mean anything by it. Night shifts are lonely, is all. He's a retiree, a widower, and he'd welcome a little human exchange. But it's clear that's not going to happen.

"If there's something I can help you with—"

She waves his words away.

So he lets her wander at will, grateful for whatever company blows in however silent; but he keeps his eye trained on the surveillance camera.

Sees her come to a halt, then disappear.

She's found the sweet spot—the one place the surveillance cameras can't track. He knows exactly where she's hiding and, although she's out of sight at the moment, it's perfectly clear to him what she's getting ready to do. That's why the cheapest items are shelved there—it's no biggie if one or two get lifted.

Only when she believes that she's safely beyond the security camera's range does Jenelle reach for the stick of beef jerky. It's a test; if the cashier calls her on it, she'll toss her few coins on the counter as proof of her honest intentions.

But nothing happens; she isn't called.

She bypasses the matches to swipe a packet of razors. It's ten to a pack, more than she'll ever need, but that's the smallest they're selling. Although she didn't plan it for this purpose, wearing cargo pants with ample pockets up and down happens to be perfect for what she's up to.

Back within camera range, she moves strangely, flopping down foot after foot, drawing attention to her movements. Working as a hospital orderly, job before this one, the cashier saw recovering stroke victims take steps like hers. She's too young for stroke, though . . . More likely, she's blissed out on something. She's heading for the toilet. He won't stop her.

She's a stunner, really good-looking. But spacey.

Is that really her own face, or a mask of her face? Something funny there . . . She cannot meet her own gaze. Her eyes avoid her eyes.

She scrapes off any remains of caked makeup with a wet paper towel. The face that comes back at her might be made of putty; it's a mask, death-gray, cratered with dark shadows. Dab of color is what she needs. She applies lipstick, then blots it *ptt ptt ptt* with a scrap of toilet paper, kissing the print of her lips—*kissing her own lips. Don't think about it!* It makes her crazy to think too much.

Eyeliner now. She's taking control. But her hand is shaky. *Soon. Soon . . . Not much longer . . .* She wants to slide to the floor, stretch out. Most of all she wants to sleep, sleep for real, but is afraid she's lost the knack. *You have to be awake first—*

She spreads out her loot on the side of the sink: pack of razors. Pack of gum. Stick of beef jerky. She'll eat—*after*. If she's still hungry. The phrase "blood meal" comes to mind.

Only the razors are truly useful.

It's like she's been bound up tightly head to foot in shrink-wrap. There's only one way to break through—

She's taking control.

What people refuse to understand is how cutting eases the panic of being so numb, brings back feeling. Pain means coming to life again.

Soon, soon. . . . Can't be soon enough.

The cellophane crackles with the sound of kindling starting to catch. Razors spill fanwise around her feet. Gleam with a blue light. *So beautiful!*

Hurry!

Before she loses her grip. Her will must be steel—unbending.

Her arms are smooth. Skin seamless, but too tight. She needs to let air in.

She hasn't done this in weeks. Time enough for the old scars to have thickened or faded away.

She'll feel better—*after.*

Where to start? Left side's easier since she's right-handed, though neither hand is working normally now . . . she cannot contain the shaking.

Jennelle strokes her inner arm, positions the razor higher than she's ever done before, starting from the blue fork where her elbow folds. *X marks the spot.* The razor so fine and light it only licks her skin. But wetness follows, whispers: *There are no promises—*

Two more strokes, ending at the wrist. *Quick*—not to pass out before she's done. The relief is immediate, overwhelming. The clarity. Emptying fills her.

Until her fingers slip. *Not working right.* Teeth chattering. *A something—something . . .* Chill like no chill she has known before. She shudders in the downdraft.

She's turning into what surrounds her, these walls, this glassy space, so cold, indifferent, *so white a darkness*, her throbbing arm—the pain is real.

The sink is spotting. *Quick!—make a splint. Make a basket . . .*
Hurry—She cradles one arm with the other. *Steady, there . . .* her
head lighter and lighter as the red petals fall drop on drop. She enters the first compartment and, without strength to shut the door,
kneels, fingers slipping into the bowl.

On the sidewall someone has written: <u>CALL ME</u>. But there is
no number to be reached, no wiped-over smudge to prove a number was ever given.

Only this for real—her fingers strengthless, water, touch water.
Call me . . .

Light gleams from the bottom of the bowl. Winks. Recedes.
Reach for it—

Gone, it's gone.

Somewhere (close by) terrible damage has been done.

Too late to undo.

Water so silken so smooth . . . so forgetful. Red, the petals continue
to drop, merge; darken.

Look:

> *how white a darkness*

34

Trew: Summing Up

Things getting rowdy, the audience closing in.

A shout: "Quit staring!"

When it happens it happens in a flash. One of the brothers swings out. Before anyone can be sure who—Josh Street or Dan Streit—started the fight, they're shoving, throwing punches, yelling, a head slamming against the tailgate—and one of them, no way to tell which without the cap, is face first in the dust.

"You freak me out—my whole life!"—hugged together with hate, as twisted and knotted up, one with the other, as head and tail end of a ball python. What nobody disputes is the fact that they're both off the truck—both out now. There's a cap on the ground—top gun no more.

And it's over—ninety-two hours! Even Trew had begun to imagine that they'd make it to a hundred, that magic number. They were so close.

Afterwards, in hindsight, people say they saw it coming: the one in the cap shifting his weight from side to side, getting ready to dodge or to strike. And the other one: how his ears twitched, like an animal's . . .

Some people say it ought never to have been allowed, two from the same family doubling the chances that one member of the family would walk away with the truck. And they were *twins*! That's about as bad as one player being handed a double chance to win.

Someone else takes immediate exception to this: "You call those two *'family'*? I wouldn't worry about sharing. Besides which—they spelled their last names different so how could anybody know? And just look where it got them! Serves 'em right . . . Things even out in the end." Another shouts out: "I hope they're satisfied. Did it to themselves—they disqualified *themselves.*"

If these remarks are intended for the brothers' benefit, they are entirely wasted. The brothers have stormed off in separate directions, not saying a word to one another, and are nowhere to be seen. Gone—disappeared—that's been the usual pattern when players drop out. Ken was an exception, but who knows where he might be by now?

As luck would have it, Vince was in the men's room when the fight broke out, which means there'll be no slo-mo footage to tease out and help settle the question of who provoked whom first. Trew's account will be the only record.

Trew has to laugh. The twins remind him of that old tale of a man granted anything he wishes, but not the usual three: one, and only one, wish is allowed. The man has no goat, but his neighbor has, and what he wants most in the world is for his neighbor's goat to die. And he gets his wish, his miserable satisfaction . . .

So the winner is Number 11: Gib the Stalwart. Whether it's by default, or earned, or fated, no one disputes his win.

Number 11 appears stunned at this sudden stroke of fortune. Spectators throng the staging area to congratulate the lucky man. The dealer, riding a final tide of emotion, declares: "These people have been through something together, and I stress the word *'together.'*" He asks for a big round of applause for *all* the contestants and for the audience as well. There are a few scattered bursts here and there: so many have left or are leaving. The dealer continues to sum up for the camera, proclaiming that what we have witnessed here is "the spirit which has made our country so envied and so great, the spirit of free enterprise and friendly competition."

It is nice to think so.

The ceremonial of handing over the keys is begun.

The winner appears dazed. Should he be trusted to drive? He needs to pause to dash some cold water in his face and take a few swigs of his coffee-coke combo.

With all his planning, Gib hadn't seen victory happening this way. And he'd been counting on feeling a little differently when it came.

But now, before the winner drives off in his trophy, Trew's got to have a word with him. A sentence will do the trick, a sound bite's enough, provided it's the right one.

What Trew gets are more words than he cares to record. Bluster and static for the most part. Everyone's frazzled and sleep-deprived, so what can you expect?

But here's the sound bite: "Basically, this is all about cool. Keeping cool over the long haul. I don't believe in chance. You make your own luck."

And Trew will run with this: It's up to you. "You make your own luck."

Trew underlines this last sentence. *Is it true? True enough? Think of self-fulfilling prophecies. True in this instance, at least?*

It will serve.

It should go down smoothly with his readers. Beyond that, Trew—along with everyone else here—is much too tired to think.

35

It's a Wrap!

Wouldn't you know it! Vince realizes he's missed the moment—the exact moment—that decided things. He'll be playing catch-up from here on out, doing his best to dance around this fact and hoping his viewers won't have been watching all that closely.

They're still announcing the winner, so maybe, Vince hopes, he isn't so far behind . . . The dealer holds the mike up close to his mouth like a lollipop, looks like he's licking it. He's got a lot of explaining to do if he means to convince people that the Street brothers simply gave up in the face of unyielding opposition and threw up their hands peacefully—and yet he's doing just that: no mention of their slugfest that gave the prize away. To hear the man talk, you'd think there'd been nothing but the friendliest sportsmanship driving this contest from start to finish.

Yet there *is* something on the upside Trew himself has witnessed—*not a big deal, but still . . .* A wife of one of the players has joined Bev—not to pray—but to embrace and weep with her. And now they're walking off, arm in arm, Bev limping, the other assisting. It's a brief moment, passing, then passed, played off the main stage, but it *is* edifying. Trew catches it, makes a note: if there's a final reckoning to be had, it has to be factored in.

There's more: Bev, abruptly, breaks free. Moving on her own now, she's veering Gib's way. When she tries to reach out it's clumsy, more lurch and grapple than the comradely hug of congratulation she surely intends. Blindsided, Gib stiffens, then quickly masks it, covering Bev's shoulder with a flurry of pats.

Yes . . . this moment too with its gesture and counter-gesture must be factored in: *the better angels of our nature, and so forth . . . It's only a moment, of course, not lasting. Give it a moment's weight, keep it short,* Trew reminds himself, *not to go overboard.*

Vince is back to routine, energized by the thought that all that's required of him now is to stay on task for the minutes remaining. The end is in sight. It can't be long now. Sleep beckons at every pause. Bed—sheer luxury—never looked so good, nor has he ever done more to earn it. So—

Full in on: people packing up. Umbrellas, folding chairs, picnic gear, coolers.

Wide shot: crowd fraying out. Tracking.

Medium close shot: winner walking towards camera, into close-up, then on past. Shooting forward: staffers clearing stage, rolling up poster, teamwork on display.

Extremely close shot: dealer handing over keys, winner fumbling them. Shit!

"Could we have that again? For the camera, please?"

Slow: repeat motion: dealer handing over keys. Winner fitting key into lock, twisting door handle.

It's like making the first cut on the wedding cake for a second time. Hokey, but it happens more often than people realize.

Winner's mugging for the camera now. "It's all good!" he announces. It's his final say.

Cab door opening. Door slamming. Winner stepping up into driver's seat, leaning out, adjusting side mirror, grinning, waving to camera. Motor gunning.

Over the hum of the motor, someone hollers: "How's she handle?"

Winner does or doesn't hear it. Gives a thumbs up. Camera rolling. . . . He's moving. He's off!

He's on his way.

Highway sounds still thin: amplify.

Turn back and widen: thinning crowd, trash, newsprint blowing.
Voice in background calling: "Sure you haven't left anything? Did
you double check?"

"Just pitch that! Over there—"

A kid totters into the frame. On his own: his mom's arms are full. He's wearing pajamas with a design of tiny trucks sprinkled on a background no longer white. He struggles to keep up with the grownups.

Everyone hollow-eyed, eager to clear out.

It's a wrap!

36

Trew: Homeward Bound

An approaching semi flashes and dips its high beams, a double blink, signaling trouble on the way.

Look out!

Here it comes.

Sure enough: Not one, but two cruisers with sirens bleating, roof-lights swirling, hurtle past in hot pursuit of—something right ahead. Trew hugs the shoulder, waiting for the commotion to subside, then inches forward.

Have to be blind not to see it—where they're heading.

It's an all-night Toot'n Totum. An ambulance waits alongside, rear doors flung wide to receive. Its lights are not flashing. The all-too-familiar elements of a crime scene come together in Trew's sideview mirror. Murder, accident, whatever . . . *Turn around?* Not for a New York minute—*not even tempted.* No, he's free, relieved to simply pass by with a blink and a nod like any other normal citizen.

No—

What's happening outside the dealership is no part of his assignment. *That's for a local reporter, a local story—*Trew has his.

Any place open 24/7 is asking for trouble.

Trew has already filed his story—the story he was sent here to write—dispatching it only minutes after the winner drove off. No loose ends, nothing inexact, a perfectly workmanlike, perfectly decent story with a beginning, middle, and end, and a touch of fable, a lesson learned, to tie up the package: "If you really want something, keep your hand on it"—verbatim quote from the winner when asked what wisdom he'd gained from having so much time to think.

And shouldn't that be enough?

His editor sounded well pleased with the piece, mentioning that the dealer had sent over a bunch of "very pretty" pictures—so many good ones that it would be hard picking out which ones to run. It's scheduled to be the lead feature in the weekend "Living" section. Trew can see it now: big spread, above the fold . . .

He's on his way to morning but not there yet. The moon remains visible, though paper-thin, a trace; darkness is fading fast. The few other cars on the road still have their headlights on—but low beam.

It's over.

Maybe it was the prospect of standing through yet one more day that rushed the contest to its close, or the very idea of a standstill race, the craziness of it finally dawning on everyone.

One way or another, it's done. Trew has his report. His theme is patience, perseverance, focus, making your own luck. Not entirely true—not flat-out untrue—but there isn't a detail to be found in it that can't be verified.

And, again, *it should go down smoothly enough. No need to keep chewing this over . . .*

One thing he'd noticed (only coming clear to him in retrospect) is how haltingly, how almost warily, the winner placed his steps when approaching the truck to finally carry it off. *Was he actually limping?* He kept on looking down, eyes on his shoes, as if the ground were cobbled, or sudden chinks and depths opening under his feet. *Terra firma not so firm as he once thought? Could be . . .*

Trew has a more immediate concern: he wonders whether it's safe for him to be driving at all. He reminds himself that he's not in his own car; this rental is newer and perkier than what he's used to.

Some music wouldn't be amiss . . . Reaching for the radio dial, he's irked to find his fingers so cramped and stiff. Country-western comes up right away, not his favorite kind, but he decides not to bother fiddling with it in hopes of finding a better station. Best to stick with whatever comes.

He's only half-listening now, anyhow, his attention fixed on the horizon, the line sharp and faintly bloodied as though drawn with a knife.

He glances at his watch (always reliable) and notices that the dashboard clock is off by an hour. *Most likely never adjusted for daylight savings. But let it be.*

The song they're airing now, as it happens, is about someone also on the road, headed for Amarillo—doesn't say by what—Greyhound, most likely. He's a bronco-buster from San Antone, making the rounds of county fairs, losing wife, saddle, and girl-friend along his way. All he owns are the clothes on his back. Not a dime to his name but he's free—he's *free!*

Pretty standard fare . . . yet irritating as ever. Trew has scant patience for that brand of freedom—or for the old folklore of the Wild West, for that matter. Texas-born, a townie, working and sav-ing all his life, he thinks of himself as native as any free-and-easy rambling cowpuncher. And—*just look around, look around*—there are more Texans riding pickups than horses nowadays. It's clear that the old ways are dying out. He's itching to change the station, but can't allow himself to shift his attention away from the road for a second and, with his hands not working right, lifting his fingers free of the wheel is a task, no longer semi-automatic. *Unsafe, to boot.* He won't touch cruise control since any adjustment there has to be made by hand.

But, really, he tells himself—*get a grip!*—and it is and isn't a laughing matter, for he's got a grip, *literally*, a grip he can't get quit of. His fingers feel sculpted to the wheel. And, anyway,—isn't it ridiculous to be so irked by a song on the radio, one that sounds like a dozen others? Besides which, the station broadcasts back-to-back and already they're onto another song about a man watching his true love two-step out the door with a stranger because of words he can't get himself to say.

He's spent, is all. *Pulped*. It doesn't help that he has no idea what his next story will be or where it will take him. It's bound to be less strenuous, though, he'll make sure of that. This one seemed a piece of cake at first, though, no way of telling in advance . . .

But what was it Heather asked him to pick up on his way back? His mind draws a blank there—only the fact that she reminded him twice; he made a promise not to forget. It's still too early to call and, besides, he's hoping it will come back to him effortlessly when thinking about something else. *Better not to have to ask.*

F amiliar sign coming up:

> DRIVE FRIENDLY
> the Texas way

Full sun now. Traffic is thickening. A dusty white pickup passes him. Motor gunning: *a statement.* All Trew can make out of the driver is the back of his head—a ten gallon hat with an upturned, smiling, brim. He must be pushing 80 or 85, *that's not friendly.* Gaping wheel-wells, *the chassis jacked up a good foot-and-a-half above the wheels. They all do this nowadays, it's not only the young ones. What's the point? To look down on everybody else? But—let them jack their heads off—those eighteen-wheeler, giant tractor-trailers, will still look down on them. So, why go to the trouble? It's just asking for a rollover, shifting the center of gravity off from where it's supposed to be . . .*

Was it potting soil? The giant size?

He has no idea.

When did he last shave? He's light-headed with exhaustion, hasn't taken a shower and only changed his socks in all the time since he started. Even his sweat is stale.

But—the contest is over, the story done.

No brooding. He shouldn't have to remind himself that this contest was only one story. New stories keep popping up all the time.
"Sufficient unto the day" as they say. The exact words escape him,
but "What's done been done" in local parlance, says much the
same thing.
    Listen:
    "I feel my heart going . . .
                     going on . . ."
Who's speaking? He hears the words as if coming from someone
sitting next to him and actually glances over to the passenger side,
knowing full well that the seat is empty. There is no other passenger. He's talking to himself.
    For, surely, it isn't the radio, where the commodities are un-
der review: slaughter cattle and grain, natural gas, crude, sweet
crude . . . *Friday, already! Hard to believe this one story has eaten up
the better part of his week.* He'll be out of commission tomorrow
and not good for anything much on Sunday.
    *It's the big Walmart after the turnoff he's supposed to stop by. For
what? What could it possibly be? Can't for the life of him—*
    *Still time, though. Won't be hitting the turnoff for eighty miles
yet . . .* Only one rough spot. Until he hits Hollarton and the riprap
of construction there, it's all blacktop, all velvet. And so far the
traffic is orderly. *Sparse and orderly. Orderly because sparse . . . Was
it dog food?* It'll come to him. *Go with the flow . . . Yes, yes, how easy
this is.* Feels like he's being carried, it's so smooth. Hands bound to
the wheel, eyes on the road—four lanes, straight as an arrow as far
as the eye can stretch—he's going home.

Notes and Acknowledgments

"Shine On Me" is a well-known spiritual. The lyrics come in many minor variants.

The refrain "yet I will pray" comes from John Bunyan's *Grace Abounding to the Chief of Sinners*. Excerpts consisting of phrases and brief paraphrases of hymns and country western songs are scattered throughout the narrative. Among them: "Amarillo by Morning," "It Is Well with My Soul," "Mansion over the Hilltop," and "The Solid Rock."

The "last words" of death row prisoners detailed in chapter 8 are based (sometimes with minimal imaginative elaboration) on the actual record of final statements available online. There has been some minor editing of this record by the TDCJ prior to filing. The presence of profanity has been duly noted wherever spoken although the words have not been transcribed in the official record; the same goes for Spanish and other non-English phrases. Should the reader be interested, the TDCJ listing can be found under the rubrics: Texas Department of Criminal Justice / Death Row Information / Executed Offenders / Last Statement. On my latest check there were 537 entries and counting, starting from 1982.

Their death certificates read "state-ordered legal homicide."

Three individuals have been helpful to me in my struggle with the raw material. Selden Hale, the distinguished Texas criminal defense lawyer, furnished books from his library. (The view of the death penalty expressed or implied here is, however, entirely my own.) I am grateful as well to Gordon Taylor and Richard Giannone who provided insightful comments on the manuscript from a literary perspective.